The Crimson Flame

Frank and Joe dangled helplessly in the air, twisting around and around until they dropped to the floor.

"Enjoy your demise," Tamm called down to them.

The boys sat stunned for a moment. They saw they were in a large, empty room made of stone blocks, with the ceiling much too high for them to reach.

Joe tried the door. "It won't budge," he said. "We're stuck!"

They moved into the center of the room, where Joe felt something slither over his shoe. He pointed the beam of his flashlight downward to the floor and froze in horror.

He was looking at a cobra!

The Hardy Boys Mystery Stories

Available from MINSTREL Books

THE HARDY BOYS ® MYSTERY STORIES

THE
CRIMSON
FLAME

Franklin W. Dixon

A MINSTREL® BOOK

PUBLISHED BY POCKET BOOKS

New York   London   Toronto   Sydney   Tokyo

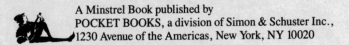

A Minstrel Book published by
POCKET BOOKS, a division of Simon & Schuster Inc.,
1230 Avenue of the Americas, New York, NY 10020

ISBN: 0-671-64286-3

First Minstrel Books printing March 1989

10 9 8 7 6 5 4 3 2 1

THE HARDY BOYS MYSTERY STORIES, A MINSTREL BOOK
and colophon are trademarks of Simon & Schuster Inc.

THE HARDY BOYS is a registered trademark
of Simon & Schuster Inc.

Printed in the U.S.A.

Contents

THE CRIMSON FLAME

1 *Bushwhacked!*

Frank Hardy looked at his wristwatch. "We have some time before our bus leaves for Bayport," he said to his brother Joe. "What do you want to do?"

"Let's go down to the World Trade Center," Joe suggested. "We can see all of New York from the top floor."

"Good idea." Dark-haired Frank led the way to the nearest subway station, and as they went through the entrance Joe suddenly grabbed his arm.

"That guy ahead of us is being shadowed," Joe whispered. "The one who looks like he's from Texas!"

Frank saw a short, stout man wearing a Western-style ten-gallon hat and cowboy boots walking rapidly toward the turnstile. Behind him was a tall, thin fellow with black hair. As the first man increased his pace, so did the second.

"I think it's a setup!" Joe declared. "That big guy's going to jump the little guy. We'd better be prepared to break it up!"

Joe, blond and seventeen, was at times the more impetuous of the Hardy boys. He liked to take chances when dealing with crooks and was ready to charge after the tall, thin man.

Frank, eighteen, tended to be more cautious. He usually wanted to investigate all the clues in a crime before plunging in. But they worked well together and they were ably trained by their father, Fenton Hardy, who had been a star detective in the New York City Police Department before becoming a private investigator in Bayport.

Frank held up a hand. "We don't have any proof that that guy's a shadow," he cautioned. "They may both be running to catch the train. Let's follow quietly and see what happens."

The two men ahead went through the turnstile and down the stairs to the platform, where they momentarily disappeared from the Hardys' view.

2

A moment later the boys heard a loud shout. "Help!" a man cried in terror from the platform. "Help me! Help me!"

Springing into action immediately, Frank and Joe bounded down the rest of the stairs, which led to the end of the platform. The last car of the train had no passengers, and its doors were open. Nobody was on the platform except the two men.

They were on the ground wrestling with each other in a wild struggle, and the man who looked like a Westerner was getting the worst of it! His tall opponent seized him by the throat with one hand and clawed at his jacket with the other!

The Hardy boys rushed toward the struggling pair. The tall man spotted them and broke free from his victim. He jumped to his feet and leaped into the train.

Joe plunged after him. *Thump!* The door slammed shut and Joe collided with it as the train began to move.

Shaken by the impact, the boy watched the subway gather speed and hurtle down the tracks. It entered the tunnel and was soon lost from view.

Disgusted, the young detective turned around. Frank had pulled the victim of the attack to his feet and was helping him to a nearby bench. Joe retrieved the ten-gallon hat, which had fallen off in the struggle. "I think this is yours," he said to the man.

"Thank you." Gasping for breath, the stranger put the hat on his head, and tilted it back, gazing forlornly at the Hardys. His big, round eyes reminded them of an owl. A small, fat owl, Joe thought. With ruffled feathers.

Just then a policeman hastened up. "What's going on here?" he demanded.

The victim regained his breath. "Officer," he exploded, "I was bushwhacked!"

The policeman looked sternly at Frank and Joe. "By these two?"

"Oh, no! These boys saved me! Otherwise I'd have been lassoed and hog-tied!"

"The guy who did it got away," Joe put in. "He's on the uptown train." Quickly he described the man he had chased.

"Maybe we can catch him at the next station," the policeman stated grimly. Through his walkie-talkie, he sent a message to his partner to phone a warning ahead of the subway train, so the patrolmen at the next stop could arrest the fugitive. Then he reached for his pen and pad. "All right, let's have the details. First, would you please all identify yourselves?"

"I'm Alfred McVay from Arizona," the short, stout man said. "I've got a spread near the Colorado River, not far from the Grand Canyon. I'm also a jewel collector. I came to New York to bid for a giant ruby at the jewel auction. I got it, too," he added triumphantly.

"Did you recognize the man who attacked you?"

"No, officer. I never saw him before. The first thing I knew, he jumped me from behind. I was seeing Arizona stars when these boys scared him off. I don't know why he did it."

"The motive was obviously robbery," the policeman said. "Maybe he knew about your ruby."

McVay smiled. "That's impossible, officer. I'm carrying the gem in a secret pocket in my coat. Nobody in New York knows about it." He opened his jacket and revealed a flap of cloth beneath his regular inside pocket. "There's another pocket under here, you see." He patted it fondly.

"The assailant may have thought the gem was in one of your other pockets," the policeman pointed out. "Anyway, it's good he didn't get it. Now, suppose you two identify yourselves," he said to the Hardys.

Frank and Joe produced their detective credentials and explained who they were.

The policeman whistled. "So you're the Hardy boys! And your father's Fenton Hardy!

5

I remember him. He was one of the best plainclothesmen we ever had on the force. I've read about the good work he's doing as a private eye. And I've heard about you boys catching a lot of crooks by yourselves when you're not busy helping him."

"Too bad we didn't catch this one," Joe said ruefully. "If the train had stayed a second longer, I'd have tackled that creep!"

"My fault, Joe," Frank apologized. "You were right when you said this guy was shadowing Mr. McVay. I hope we meet up with him again. We'll both tackle him!"

Frank addressed McVay. "Apparently he followed you, hoping to get a chance to jump you. When he saw the last car of the train empty and no one around, he had his opportunity. He probably figured he could run into the car after the attack, or escape through the subway station."

The policeman nodded. "Good thinking, Frank. Anyway, you boys deserve the credit for saving Mr. McVay. It's nice to see public-spirited citizens who are ready to come to the aid of someone in trouble. Everybody should be willing to get involved."

At that moment, the policeman's partner joined them. "Too bad," he announced. "The fugitive got away at the next station. He disappeared in the crowd before the patrolmen arrived and could nab him. But we'll put out an all-points bulletin on him. The description fits Oscar Tamm!"

The Hardys gasped. They knew from the FBI bulletins their father received that Tamm was a notorious jewel thief!

"We've been trying to catch Tamm for years," the officer, who had taken their report, lamented. "Him and his partner, Nick Summers, a medium-size guy with light brown hair and steel-rimmed glasses. You didn't see him around by any chance, did you?"

"No," Frank said. "But if we find any clues, we'll sure let you know."

"Thanks. And say hello to your dad, will you?" the policeman said before he and his partner left.

Joe scratched his head. "If Tamm was after your ruby, Mr. McVay, how did he know about it? He wasn't at the jewel auction. At least, I didn't see him."

"Were you there?" Mr. McVay asked in surprise.

"Yes. We were hired to accompany a Bayport jeweler who had a briefcase full of valuable gems to be auctioned off," Frank replied. "That's why we're in New York. But we only stayed for the diamond auction. We didn't see the ruby auction. Perhaps Tamm *was* there. He could even have been in disguise, hiding in the crowd."

"Impossible!" McVay interrupted. "There was no crowd by then. This ruby is so expensive that only five buyers were present when the auctioneer called for bids. I'd have noticed if one of my competitors had been as tall as Tamm. No, he wasn't there."

"One of the buyers might have been an accomplice who told Tamm you had the ruby," Joe observed. "Maybe Nick Summers!"

McVay shrugged. "That could be, I suppose."

Frank changed the subject. "Why did you take the risk of carrying the ruby into the subway?"

McVay winked at him. "That's the point, Frank. I figured no criminal would guess I was carrying a valuable gem if I took the subway back to my hotel. Besides, I concealed it in my secret pocket."

The Arizona rancher patted his jacket as he spoke. Suddenly he gulped and turned pale.

"I don't feel the ruby in my pocket anymore! I thought it was there before, but I must have made a mistake. It's gone!" he croaked. "It was stolen after all!"

2 Rooftop Fight

McVay looked about wildly as the Hardy boys jumped to their feet.

"We'll have to report this to the police!" Joe exclaimed.

Frank agreed. "Let's try to catch the officer we just talked to!"

The boys were about to rush off when suddenly McVay, who was frantically feeling around the inside of his jacket, called to them, "Hold it! There's no need for the police after all." He added in an apologetic tone, "The ruby just slipped down into a corner. Here it is."

He was about to pull it out when Frank stopped him.

"Not here," the boy said. "The next train is coming and the passengers might notice your valuable gem. Let's not take any chances."

Joe nodded. "You'd better get back to your hotel in a taxi, Mr. McVay. Where are you staying?"

"The Victoria Arms."

"Suppose we go with you? We can all ride together in a cab."

"That suits me," the Arizona rancher agreed. "You boys saved me from Oscar Tamm, and I'll feel safer if you accompany me."

The three left the subway station and Frank hailed a taxi. Soon they were cruising through New York City traffic toward the hotel. They discussed the sights of the city as they went uptown along the Avenue of the Americas.

In the rearview mirror, Frank noticed a green compact behind the taxi. The car trailed them block after block. He could see that the driver was a man with bushy gray hair and dark glasses.

"We're being tailed!" Frank warned in a whisper. "A guy in a green car's sticking to us like a shark following a pilot fish! I wonder what he's up to!"

McVay turned pale and his owllike eyes became as round as saucers. "He's after my ruby!"

he said in a tremulous voice. "*He* was at the auction!"

"He may be Nick Summers in disguise," Joe muttered. "We'd better lose him."

The younger Hardy rapped on the plexiglass partition separating the front of the taxi from the passenger compartment. He passed the driver a ten-dollar bill through a slot and said, "There's a guy behind us whom we want to lose. Think you can do it?"

The driver grinned. "I can sure try!" He began changing lanes to make it hard for the car to stay behind him. Then, at the right moment, he shot into a side street just before the light turned.

At this point another car had moved between the taxi and the green compact, and their pursuer was forced to stop. Joe saw him scowl furiously.

"He's plenty mad!" Joe chuckled.

"And we're lucky," Frank said. "There's not much traffic on this street. We'll be at the next corner before the light changes." He told the driver to take a route down Fifth Avenue, then across to Madison, where they continued their way uptown. By the time they reached the Victoria Arms, the green compact was nowhere in sight. The three paid the driver, entered the hotel, and took an elevator to McVay's room, which was on the twentieth floor. Pulling his key from his pocket, the man unlocked the door and led the way in.

"Sit down, sit down," he said, motioning to a sofa. Then he drew up a chair for himself. With a roguish grin, the Arizona rancher pulled his jacket open and lifted the cloth flap so the Hardys could see his secret pocket.

"That was my idea," he explained. "I had my tailor put it in." He pulled back the zipper and reached down, drawing out a small gray pouch held closed by a drawstring. He opened it and turned the pouch upside down.

A ruby fell out onto the palm of his hand. Smiling, he held the precious stone up in the sunlight that streamed through the hotel window.

"Wow!" Joe exclaimed. "It's huge!"

The ruby was indeed large, and oval in shape, with convex sides pushing outward like a slightly inflated balloon. The sunlight caused a deep crimson color within the gem, which reflected shimmering rays in a starlike pattern.

"This is the Crimson Flame," McVay announced proudly. "A king of rubies."

The Hardys were impressed. They knew a lot about rubies because they had worked on a number of jewel robberies, but they had never seen a ruby so large or quite as brilliant.

"It's a star ruby," Frank said. "It must be four carats."

McVay nodded. "You're right. It *is* four carats. It's the biggest ruby in my collection."

"And probably the most valuable," Joe suggested. "You'd have to empty more than your piggy bank to buy it!"

"It cost me a pretty penny, Joe. The Crimson Flame was found in a mine in Thailand not long ago," the rancher explained. "I learned just the other day that it was going to be auctioned off in New York. So I hurried here to be in on the bidding. Of course, I didn't anticipate being attacked by a jewel thief in the subway!"

A sudden thought struck Joe. "Mr. McVay, when you took the ruby out of your pocket just now, I noticed that the zipper was halfway open. Hadn't you closed it when you put the valuable gem inside?"

McVay stared at him. "Of course I did. I made sure the zipper was shut all the way before I left the auction." He frowned, then added, "I was alone at the time, too. No one saw me put the pouch in the pocket."

Frank recognized the point of Joe's question. "Oscar Tamm must have pulled the zipper when he was fighting with you! So he did know about the secret pocket in your jacket. He *was* after the Crimson Flame, and he almost got it!"

McVay looked puzzled. "How could a jewel thief in New York know about my secret pocket? I didn't tell anyone here about it."

"Tamm must have been tipped off!" Joe exclaimed. "Who *does* know about the secret pocket?"

"Only some of my friends in Arizona. And none of them would tell. Anyway, none of them knows Oscar Tamm. Most of them have never even been to New York!"

McVay became more and more agitated as he spoke. He blinked his eyes and stared at the Hardys.

Suddenly the phone rang. He started at the shrill noise. Dropping the Crimson Flame into its pouch, he pulled the drawstring tight and dropped the pouch into the secret pocket of his jacket. Then he jumped to his feet and ran into the bedroom. The boys heard him lift the receiver and speak in a low tone, until he said abruptly in a loud voice, "Who are you? Why are you threatening me?"

The Hardys sat bolt upright on the sofa, holding their breath and straining their ears to hear what would come next. But there was only si-

lence for a moment, then the sound of the bedroom window being pushed up.

"He can't be going out on the fire escape, can
he?" Joe wondered.

"We'd better stop him if he is!" Frank replied.

Suddenly, McVay let out a terrified yell.
"Frank! Joe!" he shouted.

The Hardys jumped up and raced into the
bedroom. The rancher was standing by the bed,
staring at the window as if in a trance, as Oscar
Tamm was climbing over the sill into the room
from the fire escape!

The jewel thief stopped when he saw Frank
and Joe. Glowering savagely at them, he
snarled, "This is the second time you've got in
my way! Do it once more, and you'll be sorry
we ever met!" He pulled back, slammed the
window shut, and disappeared.

Joe dashed across the bedroom and threw the
window open. Leaning out, he spotted Tamm
climbing down the fire escape. "He's too far for
us to catch him!" he called out.

"Let's head him off!" Frank cried, grabbing
his brother's arm. The two raced out of the room
and into the hallway. They hurried toward the
elevator, but both cars were on the first floor
and did not move when the boys pushed the
button.

"We can't waste any time," Frank said. "Let's go down the stairs." He pushed open the exit door and the Hardys took the steps three at a time, balancing themselves by grasping the railing with one hand at each leap. On the tenth floor Frank stopped. "I'm going to see where he is now," he announced.

He ran along a corridor to an open window that had access to the fire escape and got there just as Tamm was climbing down from the floor above. Reaching out, Frank caught him by the ankle, but the jewel thief, kicking furiously, broke loose and started back up.

"We headed him off!" Frank cried. "Maybe we can trap him now!"

He went through the window first in pursuit of the criminal. Joe followed. Up and up they went, steadily gaining on the fugitive, who paused to peer in each window as he passed.

"He figures he can get through an empty room and escape," Joe muttered. "I hope they're all occupied!"

"Looks like they are," Frank assured him. "Tamm's heading for the roof!"

They passed McVay's room on the twentieth floor, and, glancing in, they saw the Arizonan sitting on the bed, motionless. Too bad we can't stop to talk to him, Frank thought.

They were now so far above the street that

cars, trucks, and buses looked like toys beneath them. Pedestrians seemed like a swarm of ants on the sidewalks. The metal skeleton of the fire escape shook under the weight of the boys as they climbed even higher.

"I sure hope the guy who built this contraption knew what he was doing," Frank said nervously.

"If he didn't, we're goners," Joe agreed.

They kept on going, and gained on Tamm with every step. Frank was reaching out to grab him when the man arrived at the top and scrambled onto the roof. First Frank and then Joe vaulted up after him.

Tamm headed for a door that led to the elevator, only to be intercepted by Frank, who was sprinting across the roof. The thief turned away, took a flying leap over the skylight, and ran along the edge of the roof where only a waist-high parapet kept him from tumbling over the edge. The Hardys stayed on his heels. He veered back toward the fire escape, and Joe cut him off.

They came to a spot where empty deck chairs were lined up so residents could sunbathe. The Hardys were just catching up when Tamm seized a chair and hurled it at them. Frank tripped over it and fell onto the roof. But Joe grappled with the jewel thief and they wrestled against the parapet. In a moment they were in danger of falling over it together!

Frank rebounded to his feet and grabbed Tamm in a headlock. Now he and Joe quickly overpowered the crook, who gave up.

"Okay, you've got me!" Tamm panted. "I'll go quietly."

"You'd better!" said Frank. "We know you're Oscar Tamm, a wanted criminal."

Tamm looked startled. "How do you know that?" he asked.

"We read all about you in the FBI bulletins. You were in on the Anderson heist!" Frank replied.

He was referring to a case in which FBI agents retrieved stolen jewels and found Tamm's fingerprints, but the thief had eluded the dragnet.

"Say, who are you guys?" Tamm inquired in a puzzled voice.

"Frank and Joe Hardy," Frank replied.

Tamm frowned. "The Hardys! I've heard about you two, but I never thought you'd be after me!"

"We'll take the elevator down and turn you over to the police," Frank told him.

The three walked toward the door leading to

the elevator. Tamm was between Frank and Joe. As they passed the place where the fire escape met the roof, Tamm suddenly plunged into Joe and pushed him over the edge! Joe was falling toward the street more than twenty stories below!

3 A Crook Escapes

Horrified, Frank ran forward and looked over the parapet, expecting to see his brother's body plunging toward the sidewalk. But then he breathed a deep sigh of relief. Joe was hanging on to the fire escape!

He quickly climbed up, and Frank pulled him onto the roof.

"I grabbed hold of the railing," Joe panted, still shaking from his harrowing experience.

"I'm glad you made it," Frank said in a husky voice. "That was a close call!"

Joe nodded. "Where's Tamm?"

The boys peered around and saw the door to the elevator slam shut.

"That's where he is!" Frank cried. He and Joe ran to the door, and Frank wrenched it open. They barreled into a short corridor between the elevator and the wall.

The elevator door was already closing. Through the narrowing crack they could see the jewel thief smirking at them.

Joe sprang forward and punched the button, but he was too late. The lights on the signal board showed the elevator descending steadily.

"He got away!" Joe lamented. "We'll never catch him if we take the stairs or the fire escape down!"

"Maybe Mr. McVay phoned the hotel detective or the police," Frank observed hopefully. "Let's take the fire escape to his room and find out."

McVay was still sitting on the edge of the bed in a state of shock. Frank slapped his face and Joe poured a glass of water down his throat before he came out of his trance.

"Where am I?" he inquired.

Quickly the Hardys explained. The Arizona rancher shook his head. "I remember the voice on the phone and Tamm at the window, and that's all. No, I didn't call the house detective or the police."

"I'll do it now," Joe said. He hurried over to the phone, asked the operator to put him through to the house detective, and spelled out the facts about Tamm.

"I saw that guy go through the lobby just a few moments ago," the detective revealed. "He got into a green compact at the curb. The driver had bushy gray hair and dark glasses. They took off going east!"

"We think the driver's Tamm's partner, Nick Summers, in disguise," Joe explained. "He tailed us along Sixth Avenue until we caught on to his game and lost him in the traffic. I spotted the license number; it's PYR 763."

The hotel detective wrote down the number. "It's a stolen Ford," he stated. "I remember the number from yesterday's police bulletin. They'll find the car abandoned somewhere in New York, if you want my opinion. They always do with crooks like Tamm and Summers."

Joe put down the phone and rejoined Frank and McVay. "Tamm got away," he reported, and explained his conversation with the hotel detective.

"And it's all my fault!" McVay wailed. "If only I had notified the clerk—"

"You were in shock," Frank said gently.

22

"Who wouldn't be if suddenly a burglar climbed through the window? Don't worry about it. Tamm will be caught."

Then the boy shifted the talk to the phone call McVay had received. "Can you tell us what it was all about? Maybe something you heard will give us a clue."

"The caller was a man," McVay said. "He threatened me and said I'd better stay on the phone and hear him out or I'd never get the Crimson Flame to Arizona!"

"He was Tamm's partner, probably the guy in the green compact who tailed us," Joe inferred. "Nick Summers, if we're right. Apparently they knew where you were staying. Summers's job was to keep you on the phone so Tamm could get in from the fire escape and take you by surprise. They didn't figure on Frank and me being here."

Frank looked solemn. "Mr. McVay, someone in Arizona must have tipped off Tamm and his buddy, someone who phoned ahead while you were on the plane to New York. Do you know anyone who could have done that?"

McVay shrugged. "Lots of people knew I was coming here to buy the Crimson Flame. I don't have any secrets from my friends."

"You could have an enemy posing as a

23

friend," Joe pointed out. "Maybe he'll try to steal the Crimson Flame when you get home. He's bound to learn that Tamm failed in New York."

McVay shivered at Joe's words. "You boys are right; I won't be safe from thieves even back at the ranch. I don't know what to do." A moment later he brightened up. "Wait a minute, I have an idea. I heard you tell the policeman you're private detectives. Well, I'd like to hire you to come to my ranch and protect me."

"We don't have another case right now," Frank admitted. "But we'll have to check with our dad before we take yours, Mr. McVay."

"That's all right," the rancher declared. "I understand from your conversation with the policeman that your father may want you to help him with one of his own cases. Let me know as soon as you can."

He gave Frank a business card with the address of his ranch and his phone number. "Now I'm going straight to the airport," he confided. "I can catch a plane to Phoenix if I hurry."

"We'll go with you," Joe offered. "We have time before our bus leaves."

The Hardys and their Arizona companion went down to the lobby, where McVay paid his hotel bill. Then they caught a taxi to Kennedy

Airport. McVay looked relieved when he went through the departure gate to board his plane. He turned to wave at Frank and Joe, who were watching in the waiting area. A few minutes later the plane taxied away and was soon airborne and headed for the Southwest.

The boys made their way to the bus terminal, and an hour later were riding through the Lincoln Tunnel.

"Chet said he'd pick us up at the bus stop," Frank said.

"Oh, get ready for a slipped disk!" Joe quipped, remembering the many jolting rides they had had in their friend's old jalopy.

"I know." Frank grinned ruefully. "But it beats walking."

Chet Morton was a rotund boy who had a passion for food. Yet, he was fast on his feet and had often been of great help to the Hardys.

When the young detectives alighted from the bus, Chet was waiting. They retrieved their bags and walked outside.

"Just put your stuff in the trunk and ride with me in the front," Chet said. "I can't wait to hear about your exploits in New York. How'd it go?"

"Smoothly," Frank said. "No problems at the auction whatever. But we picked up a little mystery on the way out."

"What!"

"Move over a bit and we'll tell you," Joe said, trying to close the door on the passenger side.

Chet did, then started the motor, and the jalopy went into explosive action. It jolted forward, bounced a few times, and suddenly stalled out, throwing Frank and Joe forward.

"Sorry, fellows," Chet apologized. "The car's been giving me a little trouble lately, but I haven't been able to get it fixed yet."

Turning the key again, he stepped on the gas, and they began a bumpy ride into Bayport. The old car backfired at nearly every turn of the wheels. The motor sputtered, the doors rattled, and the tires squealed when they turned a corner. Joe braced his feet on the floor to maintain his balance. Frank gripped the back of the seat for support.

The Hardys had to speak loudly to be heard. They informed Chet about Alfred McVay, Oscar Tamm, and the Crimson Flame mystery. "We have to let Mr. McVay know if we can take the case," Joe concluded.

"I'm sure you will," Chet said, rolling his eyes. "Hey, I have an idea!" he added excitedly. "Biff and I've been looking for summer jobs, but had no luck so far. If you go out to Arizona, maybe you could find work on the ranch for us!"

Joe laughed. "We'll try," he promised.

Chet let the Hardys off at their house, then clattered away. Frank and Joe went inside and found their pretty, slim mother in the living room. She greeted her sons warmly. Their father, she said, was away on a case.

"I hope there wasn't any danger in escorting Mr. Ambers to the jewel auction," she added hopefully.

"Nothing to it, Mother," Frank responded. "It was as easy as pie."

"Pie!" said a voice from the kitchen doorway. "I've got a cherry pie in the oven."

The speaker was Gertrude Hardy, Fenton Hardy's sister.

"We sure would like a piece, Aunt Gertrude," Frank and Joe said in unison.

They went into the kitchen, where they soon were devouring cherry pie and gulping down milk.

"That's a reward for staying out of trouble this time!" Gertrude Hardy emphasized. She often spoke tartly to her nephews, but they knew she was fond of them all the same.

"Actually, we did run into some trouble," Joe admitted. "But not at the jewel auction."

"It was later, in the subway," Frank added. "A thief was trying to steal a ruby from an Arizona rancher." He told the whole story.

Their aunt sniffed. "Well, I suppose you just can't go anywhere without tangling with a criminal. If there's one around, you'll find him!"

In spite of her disapproving tone, she served them second helpings of pie. Just then the phone rang. Their mother answered it, then called out, "Frank, Joe, your father wants to speak to you."

The boys ran into the hall and took the receiver. "How did it go in New York?" the detective asked. "Did anyone try to snatch Mr. Ambers's diamonds?"

Frank chuckled. "No, but someone almost got Mr. McVay's ruby."

"Who's Mr. McVay?"

Quickly the boys described everything that had happened. Fenton Hardy listened with great interest.

"There's no reason why you shouldn't go to Arizona," he commented after hearing the details. "But be careful. Oscar Tamm is a notorious strong-arm man. Anything he's mixed up in is bound to mean trouble. Well, I'd better go. I'm keeping a suspect under surveillance." He hung up.

Joe called the airport and discovered that there was a midnight plane from Bayport to Phoenix. From there, a shuttle would take them to Flagstaff, the nearest commercial airport to the McVay ranch.

Frank then phoned the rancher. McVay sounded distraught.

"You must get here in a hurry!" he said. "Strange things have been happening!"

4   *The Sinister Foreman*

Frank was startled by the sound of the rancher's voice. "What's wrong?" he exclaimed.

"I can't talk over the phone," McVay declared mysteriously. "I'm afraid it may be bugged. That wouldn't be the strangest thing that's happened. How soon can you be here?"

"We'll catch the midnight flight, Bayport to Phoenix, and then shuttle to Flagstaff."

"Good. My foreman Wat Perkins will meet you. By the way, do you and Joe ride? Have you ever been on a horse?"

"Sure. There's a stable near Bayport and we ride whenever we can."

"Excellent. I'll introduce you as a couple of new ranch hands I've signed on. You can stay in the bunkhouse with the men. That will give you a cover while you proceed with the investigation. I don't want to say anything more. I'll fill you in when you arrive."

The line went dead at the other end. Frank relayed to Joe what McVay had said, and the two quickly packed their bags for the trip to Arizona.

"I hope you won't meet any more jewel thieves," Mrs. Hardy said apprehensively when Frank and Joe explained where they were going.

"Not if we can help it, Mother," Frank replied soothingly. "There's probably a simple explanation for the things that have happened at the ranch."

Gertrude Hardy sniffed. "Just don't fall into the Grand Canyon!"

"Don't worry, Aunty, we won't!" Frank chuckled.

Shortly after midnight Frank and Joe were airborne and heading for Arizona. After their hectic day, they slept soundly until the plane landed in Phoenix. From there, they took a shuttle flight to Flagstaff. A man in a cowboy outfit met them when they came through the gate into the waiting room.

"I'm Wat Perkins," he introduced himself, "the foreman in charge of Mr. McVay's ranch hands. I understand you boys are joining us."

"That's right," Joe said.

"Come on, I'll drive you to the ranch," Perkins went on. "Mr. McVay's at a meeting with the sheriff. He says you're to get settled in the bunkhouse with the rest of the cowboys, and he'll talk to you later when he comes back."

"Sure, Wat," Frank said. "And thanks for picking us up."

Perkins had a dusty pickup waiting. The three got into the front seat and he started off. They talked about the ranch, and the Hardys were careful not to reveal that they were detectives on an investigation.

"We're glad to have these jobs," Frank said. "We understand it's a pretty good ranch. Nothing unusual going on, is there?"

"Like what?" Perkins snapped, glaring at them. The foreman seemed annoyed.

Joe decided to distract him with a joke. "Oh, like a difficult boss, or cattle rustlers, or something like that."

Perkins started. His hand slipped on the steering wheel and he had to twist it hard to get the vehicle under control. "We haven't lost any cattle at the McVay ranch," he grated. "I don't know what's going on at the big house. I'm just a cowboy, living in the bunkhouse with the rest of the cowhands."

He gave them a sinister look as he spoke. Frank and Joe glanced at each other. They were thinking the same thing—Perkins might know more than he was telling.

He certainly acted upset when Joe mentioned rustlers, Frank thought. That's odd. Mr. McVay didn't say anything about such a problem. We have to keep our eyes on Perkins.

Suddenly the foreman pulled the pickup to the side of the road and stopped. "Something's wrong with the motor," he declared. "I'll have to look at it. Can you boys give me a hand?"

"Sure thing," Joe replied, even though the engine sounded perfectly fine to him. "We often work on our own car at home."

Perkins jumped out of the truck, strode quickly around to the front, lifted the hood, and stuck his head under it. The Hardys followed him.

"I can't figure out what's wrong," the foreman muttered. But Joe, ducking under the hood beside him, saw that a spark plug was out of place and pushed it back in. "That should do it," he said.

"I don't know," Perkins replied, shaking his head. "You boys stay here and watch the engine while I start it."

He got into the front seat and turned the ignition on. The motor roared into action, and the pickup lurched forward, heading straight toward the Hardys!

Instantly Joe shoved his brother to the side. Bowling him over, he managed to get both of them out of the way. The truck barely missed them as it roared past!

Perkins slammed on the brakes, then jumped out of the pickup. "Sorry," he cried out. "I thought it was in park—I don't know how it could have happened. I'm really awfully sorry. Good thing I didn't run you over!"

"That's all right," Frank muttered. "Don't worry about it." But to Joe he said in an undertone, "I think he did that deliberately. He probably pulled the spark plug out when he ducked under the hood so he'd have a chance to run us down."

"But why?" Joe whispered.

"I don't know, unless our cover is blown already."

They got back into the truck and Perkins drove to the ranch. They passed the big, sprawling house where McVay lived, and took a curving path around to the rear. There the Hardys saw the bunkhouse flanked by a barn, a silo, a stable, and a number of corrals for penning up livestock out in the open. They entered the bunkhouse, and Perkins introduced them as a couple of new ranch hands.

The cowboys were a friendly group, except for a pair named Barson and Marti, who seemed to be the foreman's particular friends. Perkins motioned to them to join him in a corner of the bunkhouse, where they spoke in low voices for a few moments.

One cowboy, called Jupe, was a youth about the same age as the Hardys. "I'm glad to see you," he greeted Frank and Joe. "We can ride the range together."

Perkins heard the remark. "That depends on how good they are," he sneered. "How about a lassoing competition?" he challenged Frank.

"I'm ready," Frank accepted. He was adept with a lasso because he had practiced rope tricks for a recent high school performance.

Everybody piled out of the bunkhouse. Perkins told Jupe to get on his cow pony and gallop past. As Jupe came by, the foreman tossed his lasso at the pony and missed. Jupe reversed direction and again Perkins missed. He tried a third time and finally made it.

"Frank's turn!" one cowboy shouted, and a chorus of voices supported him.

Perkins scowled. "Jupe rode too fast for anyone to lasso his pony," he complained. "Well, let's see how good *you* are!" he taunted Frank.

A cowboy handed the young detective a lasso. Coiling the rope in one hand, Frank stepped forward. "Okay, Jupe," he called out. "Ride as fast as you can!"

The youth urged his pony forward at a head-long gallop. Making circles in the air with his lasso, Frank expertly judged Jupe's speed and distance. As the pony pounded abreast of him, the young detective hurled his rope just in front of it. The lasso fell over the pony's head and circled its neck. Jupe reined his mount in and cantered back to the others, who were applauding Frank's victory.

"He'll make a good cowhand," one man declared emphatically. "He beat the boss!"

Perkins looked disgusted and said sullenly, "We'll see how good he is riding the range."

Just then the bunkhouse phone rang. Jupe went to answer it. "Frank and Joe," he called out. "Mr. McVay wants to see you!"

When the brothers entered the house, McVay met them at the door and greeted them warmly. "I just spoke to Sheriff Gomez," he said, "and asked him to keep an eye out for the jewel thieves. But he's already got his hands full with law enforcement in the county. That's why I'm glad you boys are here. The sheriff is the only one who knows you're detectives. He's coming over to meet you."

"Good," Frank said. "We like to work with the police as much as we can. But what about the strange things you mentioned on the phone? Can you tell us about them now?"

McVay gave him an owlish look. "Well, first of all, a mysterious rider has been watching this ranch from a ridge out in the desert. I spotted him yesterday. He wore a bandana over his face and a broad hat pulled down over his ears, so I couldn't identify him. He rode a gray horse."

"Obviously a disguise," Joe commented. "Did you try to catch him?"

McVay nodded. "I ordered Wat Perkins to give chase, but he came back empty-handed. Said he lost the mysterious rider in the rugged terrain out there. It's a maze of hills, buttes, cliffs, and gulches. Easy to hide in. If the intruder comes back, I hope you two can ride him down and bring him in."

"We'll try," Joe promised. "Suppose we form a posse and go after him?"

"That might be a good idea," McVay agreed. "You can take the cowboys in the bunkhouse. I'll tell them that they're to saddle up if you give the word."

"What else has happened?" Frank wanted to know.

McVay sounded upset. "Something that bothers me more than anything. The night before last, I heard a sound outside the house. I looked out my bedroom window and saw somebody sneaking through the yard. I ran downstairs and looked out the front door, from where I could see him plainly in the moonlight. He sneaked around the house and then crept toward the bunkhouse."

Frank became excited. "Who was he?"

"Jupe!"

The Hardys stared at each other. Jupe seemed like such a pleasant and honest young man!

"He may be in with the jewel thieves," McVay went on. "I think that's why he was watching the house. He's trying to see how he can steal my ruby. You'd better watch him closely!"

"We certainly will," Frank assured the rancher. "But you should not jump to conclusions. Jupe may have had another reason for acting the way he did."

McVay shrugged. "At this point, I suspect almost everyone." Then he brightened. "Would you like to see my jewel collection?"

"We'd love to," Joe said.

"Then come with me." McVay led the Hardys downstairs to the basement. His treasures were housed in a vault in the cellar, and he turned off the burglar alarm with a secret switch hidden under the stairs.

Then he twirled the dial on a heavy metal door, twisting it back and forth until he hit all the numbers in the combination. Opening the door, he entered, followed by the Hardys. An overhead flourescent light went on automatically.

Frank and Joe found themselves in a small room faced with cinder blocks on three sides. The fourth side was protected by steel bars extending from the floor to the ceiling and connected halfway up by a broad steel band running from wall to wall. The floor and ceiling were made of reinforced concrete.

A long black case stood in the center of the vault. It was composed of a riveted metal frame surrounding an oblong of shatterproof glass. The four metal legs were bolted to the floor. McVay took a key from his pocket, unlocked the case, and pushed the lid up.

"Wow!" Joe exclaimed. "What a fabulous treasure!"

Both boys were dazzled by the sparkle of five rows of jewels, including diamonds, emeralds, and pearls. A large, gleaming ruby lay on a black velvet cushion in the middle of the display.

"That's the Crimon Flame," Frank said, recognizing the stone.

"Right," McVay said. "It's the star of my collection. Did you know, by the way, that the ruby is one of the hardest jewels?"

Frank nodded. "It's made of corundum, one of the hardest minerals. Only a diamond will scratch a ruby."

"That's correct." McVay soundly faintly disappointed that Frank was ahead of him. "Well, do you know where rubies come from?"

"A lot of places," Joe interjected, "including the U.S.A. But the best rubies are found in the Far East, in places like Burma and Thailand, where the Crimson Flame comes from."

McVay blinked. "You boys know a lot," he conceded. "I'm glad you're working for me. You can see my jewel collection is well protected. This vault is practically burglarproof. I'm the only one who knows the combination to the lock or has a key to the jewel case. Yet, I'm plenty worried about thieves!"

As he spoke, they heard the sound of a fragment from a cinder block splintering underfoot in the basement corridor. Footsteps advanced toward the vault, which McVay had left open.

The rancher's eyes bulged in his owllike stare. "You see, I was right!" he gasped. "Someone's after the Crimson Flame!"

5 *The Mysterious Rider*

The Hardys sprang toward the door of the vault to confront anyone trying to get in. The footsteps came closer, and a pale man dressed in black appeared. Between the bars they could see he was carrying a heavy silver tray under his arm. He stopped when he saw Frank and Joe barring the doorway.

"Sir," he said to McVay, "Sheriff Gomez phoned to say he is tied up with a stolen car investigation. He will come here as soon as he can."

McVay relaxed. "Oh, thank you, Wilbur," he said, then introduced the man as his butler. "Frank and Joe here are our new cowhands," he added.

Wilbur raised an eyebrow, apparently surprised that his boss would show his collection to the help, then left.

McVay turned to the boys. "How are you going to proceed with the investigation?"

"The vault looks solid," Frank admitted, "but we'd better scout the rest of the basement. If crooks can get in here somehow, they'll have a shot at breaking into the vault."

McVay seemed irritated. "I wouldn't build a vault like this and leave the basement unprotected!"

"We just want to be sure we're touching all the bases," said Joe diplomatically.

The rancher agreed, then closed the jewel case and locked it. The group emerged from the vault into the basement corridor, and McVay spun the dial of the combination lock to the door. Finally he flipped the switch under the stairs to turn on the burglar alarm.

"Report to me when you've finished down here," he said as he went upstairs.

The Hardys made a tour of the basement, inspecting the walls, windows, and cellar door.

"The walls are solid," Joe declared when they met to compare notes. "Not a single cinder block is out of place. A mouse couldn't get through here."

Frank nodded. "And the door and windows

are bolted on the inside," he said. "Besides, the windows are too small for anyone to get through."

"And they have bars over them," Joe said. "That means a prospective thief would have to come through the house. It would have to be an inside job, unless the house was empty."

They went upstairs to report to McVay, but did not find him on the first floor. They noticed a spiral staircase leading to the second floor and were about to ascend when Joe happened to look up and saw a heavy metal object hurtling down at them!

"Frank, get back!" he shouted.

The boys jumped out of the way and the object hit the floor with a terrific crash. It was the silver tray Wilbur had carried when he had come into the vault!

The Hardys looked up in surprise. Wilbur was staring at them over the balustrade of the second floor. Then he hurried down the stairs.

"I must apologize," he stammered. "The tray slipped out of my hand. I hope you boys are all right."

"Sure, we are," Frank said. "But we nearly got silver-plated!"

Joe winced at his brother's pun and looked at the butler. "Where's Mr. McVay?"

"He's in his study. That's what I was coming down to tell you."

The Hardys watched the butler pick up the tray and disappear into the kitchen.

"I think he dropped that tray on purpose," Frank muttered.

Joe scratched his head. "But why? He doesn't even know us!"

They found the rancher in his study. He listened to their account of how Wilbur had nearly dropped the silver tray on them.

"It must have been an accident," McVay stated. "I have always found Wilbur to be entirely trustworthy. There's no reason why he should spy on you boys or try to get you out of the way. What will you do now?"

Frank explained. "The basement's safe, as you said. And if Wilbur's trustworthy, it would be tough for only one crook to come through the house to get at the vault. It would take a gang to hold up you and the servants."

"We'll keep your cowboys under surveillance," Joe continued. "Maybe if we ride around the ranch we'll find a clue. Let Jupe ride with us. He'll be off his guard and may let on why he cased the house the other night."

McVay nodded. "Good idea. I'll phone Perkins in the bunkhouse and tell him to let Jupe show you around."

The Hardys found everything ready when they got to the bunkhouse. They walked with Jupe to the stable, where all three saddled mounts for their ride. Frank's horse was white and Joe's black, while Jupe rode his brown and white pony. Cantering away from the stable, they saw the everyday work of the ranch going on.

The first building they came to was the barn. Some of the hands were pitching hay into the loft. Others were working the machine that carried corn on a revolving belt up into the silo.

They continued on past chicken coops and storehouses, and came to the ranch smithy where the blacksmith was shoeing a horse. Clouds of steam rose as he plunged red-hot metal into a tub of water. He laid the metal on an anvil with a pair of tongs and beat it into the shape of a horseshoe. Lastly, he fitted the shoe around the horse's hoof and nailed it firmly in place.

The three boys discussed life on the ranch. Jupe said he had always wanted to be a cowboy. "This is my first job, though," he confessed. "You fellows must be more experienced than I am. I've only been here a month."

Joe shook his head. "It's our first time, too. Maybe you can give us some pointers—how to ride the range and all that."

"I'll be glad to," Jupe said, and he talked about busting broncos and branding cattle.

Suddenly Joe switched subjects. "We hear there's something going on around here."

The young cowboy reined in his pony. "What do you mean?" he asked in surprise.

"A cowboy was traipsing around the big house the night before last. Mr. McVay saw him. Said it appeared as if the guy was staking out the place."

Jupe shrugged. "I wouldn't know. I was asleep in the bunkhouse."

"All night long?"

"Sure. What are you getting at, Joe?"

"Mr. McVay said the cowboy looked like you!"

"Oh, no, it wasn't. Why would I hang around the big house?"

"Maybe you were looking for something."

"I don't know what you're talking about!" Jupe said vehemently. "I never left the bunk-house!"

The Hardys were amazed at Jupe's self-confident bearing and his truthful appearance. Either Mr. McVay made a mistake, Joe thought, or Jupe's the smoothest liar around.

Sharing Joe's feeling, Frank decided there was no point in pursuing the matter further. He went on to a different subject.

"Have you heard about the mysterious rider on the ridge outside the ranch? The one who wears a bandana over his face?" he asked.

Jupe became excited. "Yes, I've seen him a couple of times. Wat Perkins chased him once. I don't know who he is or where he comes from, though."

Just then the trio approached a corral where a single bronco was penned up. The animal hurtled around the enclosure, bucking, snorting, and making the bars rattle as it pounded against them. Its eyes glared wildly.

"That's a mean one," Jupe said. "A wild horse we just captured. It'll take a long time to break him."

Suddenly the bronco lurched against the gate, which swung open. The horse shot out of the corral and galloped toward the open range!

Instantly, the three boys took up the pursuit. In the lead, Frank caught up with the wild horse, lifted his lasso, waved it around his head, and dropped the coil over the bronc's head. Joe, who was close behind, also lassoed the runaway. They brought the horse to a halt and led it back to the corral, where Jupe closed and locked the gate.

"Marti's supposed to make sure that the gate's closed," the young cowboy declared. "I wonder where he is?"

Just then the man came riding up. "What are you doing at my corral?" he demanded gruffly.

"The gate was unlocked and the bronc got out," Frank replied. "We brought him back in."

Marti glowered at him. "I left it locked!" he muttered, then turned and rode away.

The three boys continued out onto the range, where a number of cowboys were herding cattle, and finally turned left at a fence marking the end of the McVay property. They followed the fence to a point where they could see into the desert. Tall buttes backed by a low range of hills met their eyes. Cliffs overhung rocky gulches.

Suddenly a light flashed from the nearest ridge. A man on a gray horse was etched against the background of a blue sky. He was wearing a bandana over his face and a slouch hat pulled down over his ears!

"It's the mysterious rider!" Joe exclaimed. "Let's go after him!"

The three urged their mounts forward in a thundering gallop and took the fence in a single bound. They pounded across the desert toward the ridge, from which light continued to flash.

"He's using a mirror!" Frank called out. "Apparently he's signaling to somebody!"

The rider on the ridge heard the clattering of hooves on the desert floor. Turning his mirror toward the boys, he flashed brilliant beams of hot sunlight directly at them. The beams hit Jupe's pony in the eyes, frightening it so badly that it jolted to a stop. Then it reared up on its hind legs with a terrified whinny, took the bit between its teeth, and ran off into the desert in spite of the boy's frantic efforts to bring it under control.

Joe lit out after Jupe. It was like a horse race as Joe's black mount moved up on the cowboy's brown and white pony. The pony was a length ahead, then half a length, until finally they were running neck and neck.

Reaching out, Joe gripped the pony's bridle and pulled its head toward him. He slowed it to a walk and then brought it to a halt.

Jupe took off his hat and mopped his face. "Thanks, Joe!" he gasped. "I thought I'd end up in Albuquerque!"

Joe chuckled. "I won the race by a nose. I should have had a bet on it!"

They turned around and rode back to where they had left Frank. He was nowhere in sight!

The young detective had been quite a distance ahead of them when they were galloping across the desert, and had not noticed the incident with Jupe's pony. Instead, he had moved on, keeping his eyes fixed on the mysterious rider. The stranger saw him pound forward and

49

hesitated for a moment. Then he pulled his horse up on his haunches, turned it around, and spurred it into a leap off the ridge to the valley on the other side.

Frank bounded up the side of the ridge in time to see the mysterious rider disappear behind a butte. He raced to the butte and circled it. Now the man ahead of him was clattering along a rock-strewn gulch toward a pass between the hills.

Frank devised a strategy to catch up with the fugitive. I'll head him off at the pass! the boy thought.

Jerking the bridle with his right hand, he guided his horse up the nearest hill and over the crest, to where he could look at the pass from the other side. He rode down the hill at the same time that the gray horse came rushing through. When the man on its back saw Frank, he tried desperately to turn around and escape through the pass.

Too late! The young detective charged forward, leaped from his horse onto the stranger's, and grabbed the mysterious rider around the shoulders! He dragged the man out of the saddle and they fell to the ground with a heavy thud!

6 Rustlers

Frank and his antagonist wrestled over and over in the dust. The man's hat fell off, revealing a shock of black hair. They battled furiously until the last turn on the ground brought Frank up on top. Bracing himself on his knees, he reached for the bandana, intending to pull it off and see whom he was fighting with. But the mysterious rider caught him by the wrist, and they strained against one another, neither able to gain an advantage until Frank began to prevail. He forced his hand inch by inch closer to the bandana, over which a pair of piercing eyes glared at him. A flicker of fear appeared in them, but suddenly the man twisted his head to

51

one side and let go of Frank's wrist.

Frank plunged heavily to the ground on the other side. The man scrambled free, ran to his horse, leaped into the saddle, and galloped off through the pass. Frank's mount had wandered too far away for him to give chase. Disconsolately, he listened to the pounding of hoofbeats grow fainter and die away in the distance.

Well, here's a clue, anyway, he thought, bending over to pick up the man's hat. It was unusual, with a broad, circular, floppy brim. The label inside bore the letters *BANG*. Unable to fathom their meaning, Frank fastened the hat to his belt, then found his horse and rode back to the ridge.

He saw Joe and Jupe coming toward him from the opposite direction. When they met, each explained what had happened, and Frank held up the hat.

Joe looked puzzled and Jupe turned the hat over and over. "This sure isn't a cowboy hat," he stated. "I've never seen anything like it, and I've lived in Arizona all my life. That word *BANG* doesn't mean a thing to me, either."

"Too bad I couldn't get his bandana off," Frank lamented. "When you wrestle around with a heavyweight, you like to know who he is."

"Did you see anything at all?" Joe inquired.

"Only that he had black hair and piercing eyes. And, of course, I found out that he's a pretty tough customer."

An idea struck Joe. "Could he be Oscar Tamm?" he asked. "He has black hair."

Frank shook his head. "This man wasn't as tall as Tamm."

"Who's Tamm?" Jupe asked.

"Oh, some guy we met in New York," Frank said evasively. "Anyway, I wonder to whom the mysterious rider was signaling?"

"There's no telling," Joe said. "If we see him again, maybe we'll be able to figure out what he's up to. Any ideas about it, Jupe?"

The young cowboy pursed his lips thoughtfully. "You know as much as I do, Joe."

They rode back to the ranch and stopped at the bunkhouse. Perkins was the only one there.

"Where have you guys been?" he snarled. "It couldn't have taken you that long to ride around the ranch."

The three took turns describing what had happened since they left the bunkhouse.

"Forget the mysterious rider," the foreman growled. "And his hat. We got work to do. Frank and Joe start tomorrow. Jupe, you come with me now. We'll help herd the cattle on the range."

Perkins and Jupe rode off. The Hardys went

into the bunkhouse and threw themselves down on their beds.

"We really don't know any more than we did before," Joe said. "What do you think about Jupe? He says he wasn't at the big house the other night, yet Mr. McVay insisted that he was."

"He could have tricked us today," Frank agreed. "Maybe he turned his pony's head toward the mirror so it would get frightened and run away. Perhaps he figured we'd ride after him, and the mysterious rider would have a chance to escape."

Joe nodded. "They could be working together. But we have no evidence against him, Frank."

"Or against Perkins, or Wilbur," Frank ticked off the list of suspects. "This is going to be one tough case!"

Suddenly he jumped out of his bunk and placed a finger on his lips in a gesture of silence. Stepping over to the wall on one side of the rear window of the bunkhouse, he motioned Joe to do the same on the other side. "Somebody's coming!" he whispered hoarsely.

They heard furtive footsteps approaching through the underbrush. There was the sound of hushed conversation as if the speakers did not want to be heard. The bushes parted and Barson and Marti appeared. They looked warily around as they moved forward.

"Wait a minute," Barson said suddenly. "I'll see if the Hardys are around."

He walked over to the window. Frank and Joe pulled back and flattened themselves against the wall. Barson shaded his eyes and peered into the bunkhouse for a moment and then turned away. "We're safe," he told Marti. "They ain't here. I guess they got lost on the range."

"My wild bronco should have run 'em down!" Marti snorted. "I left the gate open so it would get out. I figured they'd spend the day chasing it and be out of our way! But they were too quick with their lassos, confound 'em! They brought the bronc back in no time flat!"

"Forget it for now," Barson counseled. "We have to get out to the main trail."

They went into the bushes and a moment later were lost to sight. Frank motioned to his brother.

"Come on, we'll follow them!"

The boys ran out of the bunkhouse and around to the rear, where they had last seen the two cowhands. The sound of breaking twigs guided them and they advanced rapidly enough to catch sight of Barson and Marti far ahead.

The two went past the corrals and through a part of the McVay range that the Hardys had not seen yet. Frank and Joe made it across the open space by ducking down and sneaking through a herd of cattle. Then Barson and Marti climbed the fence and vanished into the woods.

The young detectives followed as quickly as they could without being heard by the two men. The path snaked through the woods, which allowed the Hardys to move closer by hiding behind the trees. When Marti turned around suddenly, they froze behind a tall pine until they heard him continue onward.

At last they came to a glade where a dirt road marked by tire ruts led through the woods. Barson and Marti stopped and looked down the road expectantly. Frank and Joe hit the ground and crawled through the underbrush until they gained the cover of a large spreading bush. They could hear the two men talking, and by parting the branches of the bush, they saw the ranch hands sitting on a log by the side of the road.

Barson was speaking. "What are the Hardys doing here at the ranch? That's what I want to know."

"Doesn't matter," Marti declared. "They'll never cotton on to our racket."

Frank and Joe listened with pounding hearts and bated breath. Marti was about to say something when a rustling in the underbrush near the young detectives brought him and Barson to their feet.

"Somebody's hiding behind that bush!" Marti rasped. He drew a pair of cowboy pliers used for fence repairs from his belt. Barson picked up a thick branch and waved it like a club. The two advanced menacingly toward the boys' hiding place, and were only a few yards away when a rabbit scooted out from behind the bush. Quickly it hightailed down the dirt road.

"A bunny!" Barson laughed and tossed his club aside. "And I almost thought—"

He was interrupted by the sound of a motor, and both men walked toward a cattle truck rounding a curve in the road. It jounced through mudholes until it reached them and came to a stop. The driver turned off the engine, then got out.

"Is everything set?" he asked. "We won't run into any hitches, will we?"

"Everything's right as rain, from here to Flagstaff!" Barson gloated. "No problem."

"You take care of your part of the operation, and we'll take care of ours," Marti added.

Eagerly, Frank and Joe waited to learn what the operation was. But all the driver said was,

"The trail's okay. We can use it." He got into the truck, circled through an open space in the woods, and drove back down the road and out of sight.

While the two cowboys watched him disappear, Frank and Joe slithered away from the bush, got to their feet, and hurried through the woods to the ranch. They were working on their cowboy gear in the bunkhouse when Barson and Marti arrived.

"How are the cattle doing out on the range?" Frank inquired casually.

"Cattle I herd always do just fine," Barson said contemptuously. "Wait till I get you guys out there! I'll show you what it takes to be a cowboy!"

Joe pretended to be enthusiastic. "You'll be doing us a big favor!" he stated.

Barson scowled at the satirical remark, but said nothing more. He and Marti went to their bunks and started working on their own gear.

A moment later the phone rang. Frank answered it. "Mr. McVay wants us to go to the big house for dinner," he called to Joe. "Seems that new ranch hands always get invited the first night."

Marti looked up from a boot he was polishing. "Enjoy your meal!" he said, but his expression was anything but friendly.

At the house, the Hardys met a neighboring rancher named Jake Jomo. He was as fit as an athlete, had brown hair, and wore horn-rimmed glasses.

"Jake's a good friend of mine," Mr. McVay informed the Hardys after the introductions were over. "He's also great on a horse. I wish I could ride as well as he can."

Jomo grinned. "Just don't let your horse step on you!" he said. "This is what mine did to me."

He held up his right hand and wrist, which were bandaged. "My horse threw me," he explained, "and my hand came down under his hoof."

After dinner, when they all were relaxing in the living room, Jomo said to the Hardys, "Since you boys are the new cowhands here at the McVay ranch, I advise you to keep your eyes open when you're out punching cattle."

"What for?" Joe wanted to know.

"Rustlers!"

"We didn't know there were rustlers anymore," Joe countered.

"Didn't they go out with the horse and buggy?" Frank inquired.

Jomo scratched the bandage on his hand. "Well, they're a different breed nowadays," he admitted. "For one thing, they're simply called cattle thieves. They run a few longhorns off the range at a time, and take them away by truck. I've lost some already, so I asked Sheriff Gomez if he can't put a stop to it."

"The sheriff's coming here this evening," Mr. McVay announced. "You can ask him how his investigation is getting along. By the way, I haven't lost any cattle to the rustlers," he added.

He had hardly finished speaking when the doorbell rang. Wilbur opened the door and announced, "Sheriff Gomez."

The sheriff was a thickset Chicano with black eyes, black hair, and brown skin. After talking to Mr. Jomo, he shook his head and confessed that he had not yet found a clue to the rustlers.

"Why don't you check illegal cattle dealers in Phoenix?" Jomo suggested.

"I've been watching Phoenix, but nothing's turned up yet," the sheriff replied. "Maybe you should hire a couple more cowboys, Jake. After all, you're undermanned. Two more men could help protect your cattle."

Jomo agreed. "I've thought of that. Trouble is, I've got to have hands I can trust, and I'm afraid any local cowboys I hire might be in cahoots with the rustlers!"

Frank had an inspiration. "Mr. Jomo, we have

two friends back home who are looking for summer jobs. They're Chet Morton and Biff Hooper. Joe and I can vouch for them!"

"That sounds like a good idea to me!" Mr. McVay said. "Why don't you give them a try, Jake?"

"Okay," Mr. Jomo said, getting to his feet. "Tell them I'll give them the same chance Mr. McVay is giving you. Have them fly out as soon as they can. Now I'd better be getting home."

"I'll call our friends," Joe offered.

"You can use the phone in my study," Mr. McVay offered.

The two boys went upstairs and Joe dialed the Morton farm near Bayport, while Frank listened in at the receiver. Chet answered.

"Oh, it's you," he said with a yawn. "Why are you calling me at this time of night? Don't you know it's bedtime back here in the East?"

"Well, I can call tomorrow," Joe said casually. "I've nothing to talk about except ranch jobs for you and Biff. No need to discuss it now. Bye!"

"Hey!" Chet yelled. "Don't hang up. Tell me about the jobs!"

Joe laughed and explained that Mr. Jomo was looking for help. "He wants you to report directly to his ranch as soon as you get here," the young detective said. "Since his place is plagued by rustlers, we recommended that he hire you so you can check out what's going on."

Chet got all excited. "That's great!" he cried. "Just what we wanted."

"You don't sound sleepy anymore," Frank spoke up.

"Sleep? Who said anything about sleep?" Chet roared. "I'll call Biff and we'll be on our way to Arizona as soon as possible!"

7 *Bunkhouse Jamboree*

Joe hung up and grinned at his brother. "I figured he'd wake up!"

Frank looked thoughtful. "It's a good thing they're coming," he said. "Maybe they can be helpful to us since our cover was obviously blown right from the beginning!"

Joe nodded. "I have a feeling Perkins knew exactly who we were when he picked us up from the airport. That would explain his act with the truck!"

When the boys returned to the living room, Mr. McVay and Sheriff Gomez were discussing how to keep thieves from getting at the Crimson Flame.

63

"Who exactly knew that you hired us?" Frank asked the rancher.

"No one but the sheriff and me," McVay replied. "I didn't even tell my friends."

"I'm glad you two are working on the ruby case," the sheriff said. "Let me know at once if you find any clues."

"We will," Frank promised. "So far, we've come up with a few interesting facts."

"Such as?"

"Well, Jupe denies he sneaked around this house the other night."

"But I saw him!" McVay exploded. "He must be in with the crooks! You'll have to watch him carefully!"

"Anything else?" the sheriff queried.

Joe looked somber. "It seems our cover's been blown. Barson and Marti are suspicious of us. We don't know why, though. Perkins must be in on it because he's thick as thieves with those two. Besides, he nearly ran us down on the drive from the airport to the ranch. We think he did it deliberately."

McVay and Gomez listened in amazement as Joe described the incident with Perkins and the pickup.

"Perkins, Barson, and Marti are three of my best cowboys," McVay protested. "You'll have to produce the proof before I'll believe they're doing anything wrong. What else did you find?"

"We saw the mysterious rider!" Frank said. "I even got my hooks on him."

"You mean you brought him in?" the rancher exulted.

Frank shook his head. "Sorry, Mr. McVay, we had some rough-and-tumble at the pass, but he got away. However, he left this," Frank added, drawing the floppy hat from his jacket pocket.

McVay examined the hat and handed it to Gomez. "I've never seen anything like it," he said.

The sheriff inspected the letters on the label. "I don't know what *BANG* means," he admitted as he returned the hat to Frank. "If you boys figure it out, you may have a lead to the mysterious rider."

After discussing the problem for a few more minutes, Sheriff Gomez left in his patrol car and the Hardys walked back to the bunkhouse.

They found the cowboys gathered together in the middle of the room. Three were plunking banjos and tightening the strings of the instruments. Two more were making shrill sounds on their fiddles. A number of other instruments were scattered around, and Jupe was blowing into a harmonica.

The young cowboy lowered the harmonica

65

and grinned at the Hardys. "We're having a jamboree," he announced. "Want to join in?"

"You bet we do!" Joe replied enthusiastically. "We play guitar."

Jupe went to a closet, rummaged around among the spare instruments, and pulled out two Spanish guitars, which he handed to Frank and Joe. The Hardys tuned up with the rest, and a hand-clapping, foot-stomping jamboree began.

The cowboys sang Western songs about riding the range and herding cattle. The fiddlers took the lead in a lament for those lost on the trail, and then the banjos broke into a sprightly air about a tenderfoot who tried to be a cowboy although he never learned to ride a horse.

"Frank and Joe!" Jupe called out after they had finished. "Let's see what you can do!"

The Hardys moved into the center of the circle carrying the instruments he had given them, and strummed their guitars to get the beat going. Their audience began a rhythmic clapping in time with the music. Then Joe started to sing:

> When the wagon train is rolling
> And your gun is by your side
> When you reach the Rocky Mountains
> And you cross the Great Divide

Then you know you're in the West
And you know that's where you'll bide.

He sang two more verses, then repeated the song while the cowhands joined in. The bunkhouse rang as the chorus of voices grew louder and there was enthusiastic applause at the end.

"Great performance!" one cowboy burst out. "You guys are real pros!"

The Hardys bowed and moved back into the circle. A side-long glance told Joe that Perkins, Barson, and Marti were up to something. Perkins jerked his thumb toward a corner of the bunkhouse, walked over, and the other two joined him. They put their heads together and talked in undertones.

Edging close while pretending to tighten the strings of his guitar, Joe heard Perkins say, "These kids are a real problem. The fact that they're becoming a hit with the other guys isn't going to help us get rid of them, either." Marti said something, but the rising roar of a sing-along prevented Joe from hearing it. He moved back to the group and pulled Frank gently by the sleeve.

They went outside and strolled a few yards away from the bunkhouse, while Jupe performed on his harmonica again. Joe repeated what he had heard. "We'd better be careful," he concluded. "They've got it in for us!"

"I'd like to know how they figured out who we are," Frank mused.

"Our pictures have been in the paper quite often," Joe said. "Maybe Perkins recognized us."

"I suppose so," Frank said.

They went back into the bunkhouse and rejoined the jamboree. Shortly afterward, the festivities broke up and the cowboys drifted away to their bunks. Perkins, as foreman, saw that they were all in bed and then snapped out the overhead light.

In the middle of the night, Frank was awakened by a stealthy sound. Raising his head and peering through the darkness, he noticed Jupe standing up and slipping into his clothes.

Instantly Frank pushed the mattress of Joe's bunk above him. His brother stirred, turned his head, and watched as the young cowboy put on his boots and tiptoed out of the bunkhouse. Quickly the Hardys threw on their own clothes and followed. By the time they got outside, Jupe was twenty yards ahead, walking slowly toward the big house.

He paused at the front door and appeared to be surveying it. Then he moved around to the right and walked along the side of the house to the back. The Hardys, peering around the corner, saw him stop at the basement door and reach the doorknob.

"He's trying to break in!" Joe said in a hoarse whisper.

"He must have cased the house the other night to find the easiest way to get in," Frank whispered back. "We'd better stop him!"

The young detectives rushed forward. "What's the matter, Jupe?" Frank asked. "No key?"

The boy gave no answer. Instead, he kept turning the doorknob and attempting to push the basement door open.

"Come on, Jupe," Frank went on. "Give up. You won't get the Crimson Flame."

Jupe still made no reply. He kept trying to force the door open with slow, mechanical motions of his arms.

"Something's fishy!" Joe muttered. Taking a pencil flashlight from the miniature detective kit he always carried in his pocket, he flashed the beam into Jupe's face.

The cowboy's eyes were closed, and his breath came in shallow gasps. His arm was extended stiffly forward and his fingers held the doorknob in a convulsive grip.

"He's sleepwalking!" Joe exclaimed.

Suddenly a light went on in the bedroom

above. The window banged open and McVay leaned out, looking at the three boys.

"Thieves! Thieves!" he yelled. "They're trying to steal the Crimson Flame! Wake up, everybody, and get downstairs. We'll bush-whack 'em!"

The noise made Jupe wake up with a start. "Where—where am I?" he mumbled.

Quickly the Hardys explained. Jupe looked sheepish. "I don't think I've w-walked in my sleep since I left home," he stammered. "But maybe the old habit is coming back."

The three went to the front of the house just in time to see the porch light flash on. McVay came out swinging a branding iron. Wilbur, in a dressing gown, carried a poker. The rest of the servants, yawning and rubbing their eyes, crowded behind them.

"Why, it's Jupe and the Hardys!" McVay exploded. "What's the meaning of this?"

Frank explained how they happened to be there. "I think Jupe was telling the truth when he said he wasn't up here the other night when you saw him. He never knew what he did because he was sleepwalking. Same as tonight."

McVay simmered down when he heard the details. He herded his staff back into the house and the lights went off one by one.

Joe, Frank, and Jupe walked back to the bunkhouse. Outside, Joe slipped a lasso over Jupe's wrist and pulled it tight. "Rope yourself to your bunk," the younger Hardy boy advised. "That way, you'll wake yourself up if you try to walk in your sleep again."

"Good idea," Jupe said. "This habit of mine is very embarrassing."

"Don't worry about it," Frank said. "Lots of people walk in their sleep. It's just that most of them don't upset Mr. McVay," he added with a chuckle.

The three went quietly into the bunkhouse so as not to wake the other cowboys, regained their bunks, and went to sleep.

At daybreak, Frank and Joe went out of the bunkhouse with the rest of the cowboys to get their orders from Perkins.

"Jupe, you work the bronco corral," the foreman barked. "Frank and Joe, you'll herd cattle this morning. This afternoon you'll ride the range and repair the fences. Now, saddle up!"

The boys went to the barn, led their horses out, and put the saddles on. They were tightening the girths that held the saddles in place when Perkins came up to inspect them. The

Hardys held their mounts by the bridle, while the foreman walked around the horses checking the stirrups, fingering the girths to see if they were tight, and tugging at the saddles.

"He's trying to find something wrong," Frank murmured to Joe. "He hopes he will."

"I bet he'd love to have an excuse to fire us," Joe agreed.

Perkins came around to where the Hardys were holding their horses head to head. "You guys saddled up okay," he admitted grudgingly. "But I doubt that you really know how to ride."

"They sure do!" said Jupe, who was standing by with his cow pony. "Joe caught up with me when my pony ran away on the desert. And Frank rode down the mysterious rider."

The foreman scowled.

"He didn't bring back the guy, did he?"

"That makes two of us," Frank suggested quietly. "Mr. McVay told us you didn't catch him either. You lost him out in the hills. I came closer than that. Anyway, we know how to handle horses."

"Show me how well you can ride!" Perkins scowled.

Frank and Joe at once leaped into their saddles, prepared to put on a riding display for the foreman. But Joe's formerly obedient horse turned into a savage bucking bronco! It reared, kicked, and twisted in a wild effort to throw him off its back!

8 *The Thundering Herd*

Joe clutched the reins with his left hand and extended his right arm to one side to keep his balance!

The horse came down stiff-legged, attempting by this maneuver to jar him loose from the saddle. Feeling the boy's weight still on its back, the animal began to buck again in an outburst of violent energy. Yet, Joe stayed in the saddle despite the bucking and tried to calm the animal down.

At last he jumped to the ground. The horse stopped bucking and looked quietly at him.

Joe scratched his head. "There's no use trying to ride him. I can't figure it out. He didn't give me any trouble before, but there's something strange about him today."

Perkins leered at Joe. "Maybe you're not as good at riding as you think, and the horse knows that now. He wants a real cowboy on his back!"

Frank, who was looking at Joe's saddle, suddenly dismounted. "I think I can explain what happened," he said. He pulled up the back of the saddle and pushed his hand under it. He withdrew a large, spiky burr.

"This is what caused it," he said. "The horse wasn't trying to throw you, Joe. He wanted to get rid of the burr sticking into his back." Frank turned to the foreman. "Perkins, you did this. You pushed the burr under the saddle while you were pretending to inspect it!"

"Go on, you're crazy!" the foreman snarled. "The wind must have blown it there!"

"Not likely!" Joe said. "It wasn't there when I put the saddle on."

The Hardys were thinking the same thing: Perkins was again trying to get rid of them, but they still had no proof against him. They swung back up into their saddles, and this time Joe's horse obeyed him when he tugged on the reins. As they cantered away from the stable, the foreman stared angrily after them.

Arriving at the range, Frank and Joe found two other cowboys already there. Barson was in charge, and he rode over to them. "We're herding these longhorns down to the corral at the ranch," he said. "You guys'll be on either side up at the front. Now, get 'em out!" With that, he returned to the rear of the herd.

The longhorns began to move, bellowing loudly, tossing their horns, and tearing up chunks of earth with their hooves. The Hardys rode back and forth, guiding the leader of the herd toward the corral so the others would follow.

Suddenly a maverick bolted away toward the open range. Joe galloped in pursuit, overtook the stray, and rode across its path, forcing it to veer to one side. It tried to get past, but again he headed it off, and it had to change direction.

Waving his cowboy hat and shouting, he chased it back toward the herd, which was moving slowly across the range.

Frank spotted another animal getting too far ahead of the others. He galloped forward to slow it down. Just when he was in front of the entire herd, Barson gave a piercing yell at the rear, and the longhorns stampeded forward!

The sound frightened Frank's horse. It stumbled as it attempted to turn and the boy fell off right in the path of the longhorns!

Horrified, Joe watched the lowered horns aimed directly at his brother. Hoofbeats pounded toward him as the runaway cattle swept over the area. He saw Frank's horse standing in the midst of the thundering herd, but there was no sign of the boy anywhere!

When the last of the animals had passed Frank's horse, it was still there, its saddle empty. Terrified, Joe rode over and looked around.

Suddenly, he heard Frank's voice. "Here I am!"

Joe stared underneath the horse. There was his brother, clinging to the girth strap!

Frank let go, tumbled to the ground, and remounted, still trembling from his terrifying experience.

"Are you okay?" Joe asked anxiously.

"Fine," he said, his voice not quite steady yet. "Not a horn touched me. Let's go back to cowpunching."

The Hardys rode forward and caught up with the herd. Resuming their old positions in the lead, they guided the first animals into the corral. The rest followed, and Frank closed the gate.

Barson rode over. "Why did you guys leave

your posts out on the range?" he demanded harshly.

"Why did you yell at the longhorns when I was in front of the herd?" Frank countered. "You knew you'd frighten them into running at me. I'd have been squashed into the turf except for my horse!"

Barson shrugged. "All I knew was you weren't where I told you to stay. I yelled at the longhorns because they were moving too slowly."

He rode off without saying anything more. The boys went to the bunkhouse and joined the other cowboys for chow. Juggling a plate of food, Jupe came up to them and they all sat down under a tree away from the others.

"I heard you almost got run over by the longhorns," Jupe said to Frank.

"Because of Barson," Frank replied. "He yelled at the herd and my horse stumbled."

Jupe nodded. "So I'm told."

The three munched on their food until Joe spoke.

"We think Barson yelled at the longhorns deliberately so they'd run at Frank. Has he ever tried anything like that with you?"

Jupe set down his plate. "No. But I once saw him and Marti out at the main trail, and he said

78

if I ever rode that way again he'd have me thrown off the ranch."

Joe became excited. "What was he mad about, Jupe?"

Jupe shrugged. "Search me. I heard voices and thought they might be rustlers. That's why I went out there. I told him that and that's when he blew his top. I guess he doesn't like being mistaken for a rustler!"

Perkins interrupted the conversation by ordering the three boys back on the job. "And you Hardys better see that the fence is repaired."

The Hardys remounted and rode out on the range. They discussed what Jupe had told them.

"Could Barson and Marti really be rustlers?" Frank wondered. "That would explain why we saw them with a cattle truck at the main trail. They may have been planning a job!"

"But Mr. McVay doesn't believe it," Joe commented. "And we can't blow the whistle on them because we have no proof. We need something more to go on."

They rode along the fence until they came to a place where a strand of barbed wire was broken. Frank dismounted and donned a pair of thick leather gloves. Then he drew the two ends of the wire together and held them, while

79

Joe used a pair of pliers to make a splice. Frank pulled the wire forward and allowed it to snap back. "Strong enough," he judged.

They continued along the fence until an open space caught Joe's eye. "Say, Frank, there's a real break," he called out. "We'll have to fix that, or Perkins will be after us for sure!"

As they approached, they saw two posts ripped out of the ground and leaning toward the underbrush on the other side. Only the sagging barbed wire prevented the posts from falling.

"How could that have happened?" Frank puzzled. "Those posts weren't broken, hacked, or sawed. They were pulled straight up and out. You can see earth stains at the bottom."

"The rustlers did it!" Joe exclaimed. "They ran cattle off the range through here and took them away by truck. They intend to come back and push the posts into the ground so nobody will be the wiser. Except now we'll lay an ambush for them!"

Frank shook his head. "I don't think so. Nobody could run longhorns through that much barbed wire. The rustlers would have had to cut it. Besides, we heard Mr. McVay say he hasn't lost any of his herd. I don't know what happened here, but it's another repair job for us."

They dismounted again, carried the posts to

the holes where they had stood before, and were about to anchor them when a movement in the sky caught Joe's eyes. He looked up.

A towering column of dust and air was coming toward them. Broad at the top, and tapering down to a point near the ground, it twisted around and around like a moving funnel. On and on the whirlwind came, tearing at trees and bushes, and churning up debris.

"It's a twister!" Joe cried. "A tornado! And it's coming right at us!"

9 Ruby Robbery

The Hardys let go of the fence posts.

"We'll have to take cover in the woods!" Frank cried.

He and Joe leaped back into their saddles. Urging their horses forward, they took the fence in long, flying jumps that carried them into the underbrush on the other side. They rode into the woods, dismounted in a pine grove, and tied their frightened horses to branches. The animals snorted, reared up on their hind legs, and pawed the air with their front hooves.

Through the branches Frank and Joe could see the whirlwind hurtling toward them. The

trees waved wildly overhead. Bushes torn up
by the roots were thrown into the branches, and
sagebrush rolling before the wind became
stuck in the barbed wire of the fence.

The Hardys hit the ground and covered their
heads with their hands. The force of the wind
grew stronger, filling the sky with dust. Trees
crashed in the woods around them.

Suddenly the tornado changed direction and
veered across the range, moving up and down
as it went. Leaping over the ranch buildings,
the churning whirlwind landed in the desert
and careened away into the wide-open spaces.

The trees stopped shaking and the horses settled down. Frank rose to his knees. Wheezing
and coughing, he rubbed the dust from his
eyes.

"Wow!" he exclaimed. "I thought we'd be
swept up and blown all the way to Mexico!"

Joe gave no answer. He was lying motionless
with his eyes closed underneath a mass of
green branches. A pine tree, uprooted by the
tornado, had fallen right next to him!

Frantically, Frank grabbed the top branches
and tried to pull the tree aside. It was too heavy
for him to move, however, so he hurried to his
horse and withdrew a pair of shears from his
gear. He attacked the tree furiously, snipping

off the branches that covered his brother.

Joe opened his eyes. "Wh-what happened?" he gasped.

"You were conked by a tree. How do you feel?"

Joe stood up shakily and felt the back of his head. "Ouch!" he winced. "I have a bump as big as a pine cone. But that's about it."

"Do you want to go back to the bunkhouse and lie down?" Frank asked.

"Naw. I'll be okay. Let's go back to work."

They untied their horses and rode to the fence. They lifted the posts again and thrust them deep into their holes, pounding them into place with mallets. Then they stamped the earth down around the base of each post.

"That should do it," Joe stated. "At least till the next tornado comes through."

The Hardys continued their ride along the fence without discovering another stretch of the barbed wire that needed repairing. Finally, they turned and rode back to the ranch. There, everything was in a turmoil because the tornado, in vaulting over the buildings, had battered them. The cowboys were cleaning up broken glass, broken shingles, and other debris at the bunkhouse. The Hardys offered to pitch in and help.

"That's not necessary," Jupe informed them. "We've got everything under control. Anyway, Mr. McVay said for you to report at the big house soon as you came in. Perkins is up there now."

Everybody from the big house was out in the front yard when the Hardys arrived. The servants milled around whispering to one another. Perkins and Wilbur were off to one side talking in low tones. McVay stood in the middle of the yard, staring up at the roof where some shingles dangled over the edge.

"I had to clear the house," McVay informed the Hardys, "for fear it would collapse. Wilbur says the tornado may have undermined the structure. We're all leery because a house on a nearby ranch was knocked down by the last twister."

Wilbur walked up, nodding his head. "That's right, Mr. McVay. Nobody should go inside until we have an inspection by the authorities."

"There's no need to wait that long," Joe said. "Frank and I will go in and see if anything's wrong."

"That would be too dangerous for you boys!" Wilbur protested.

Frank turned to the rancher. "We've worked for a builder once and we know how to look for signs that make a structure unsafe. Believe me, we won't take any unnecessary chances."

McVay shrugged. "Since you're experienced, you might as well," he agreed. "I'd rather not wait any longer than I have to."

"I'll come along," Wilbur offered quickly. "Three will be better than two in case of an emergency."

McVay was grateful. "Thank you," he said. "It's good of you to take the risk."

The Hardys thoroughly checked the foundation for cracks before going inside. Then they went into the living room, with Wilbur following close behind. The windows on one side were shattered, and the tornado had overturned several chairs. Frank and Joe circled the room, tapping on the walls and sounding the floor with their heels. They looked up the fireplace where a pile of black dust had fallen into the grate.

"This room is solid," Joe commented. "But the basement may not be."

"It's unnecessary to go into the cellar," Wilbur spoke up. "The cinder blocks cannot be damaged."

"You never know, Wilbur," Frank said. "We have to make sure."

The butler shrugged as if to say he did not care, and accompanied the boys into the basement. They found all the cinder blocks intact.

The windows were unbroken, still bolted, and the bars over them held firm when Joe shook them. The jewel vault looked exactly as they had seen it before.

"Seems to be okay," Frank said. "Now, hold your ears!" Gripping the dial of the combination lock between his fingertips, he twirled it sharply. At once, the deafening wail of a siren broke out, filling the basement with its shrill sound.

Joe placed his palms over his ears. "Stop it, Frank," he implored, "or we'll all go deaf!"

Frank pulled his hand away and the noise ceased. "I wanted to see if the burglar alarm still works," he explained.

Wilbur glared at him, but did not comment.

They went upstairs again and looked the building over from the ground floor to the attic. They found no structural damage, only debris here and there left by the tornado.

Joe leaned out the attic window to inspect the area where the shingles were torn loose. "I think this can be fixed without much trouble," he said, bending down as far as he could to feel the roof.

"Let me see," Wilbur said. He pushed closer, and in doing so, bumped into Joe's precariously balanced body!

With a yell from the boy, his legs lifted up

and he slid out the window!

Frank ran over but could not halt Joe's fall in time. Flailing wildly with his arms, the younger Hardy managed to grip the gutter and came to a stop. Pale and shaken by this frightening incident, he carefully got up, made his way back up the roof, and climbed into the window.

"Are you all right?" Frank asked, his heart still beating violently with fear.

"Yes, sure." Joe stood for a moment to catch his breath, then turned to the butler. "I seem to be accident-prone when you're around," he said as evenly as he could. "First you drop a silver tray on me, then you shove me out the attic window. Would you mind staying away from me from now on?"

"It—it was an accident!" Wilbur stammered. "Believe me, I had no intention to harm you in any way."

Frank looked at him, not believing a word.

"Let's cut out those accidents in the future, or you may get into real trouble!" he said grimly.

Wilbur did not reply. When they were downstairs again, he tried to act as if nothing unusual had happened. "I suggest we take another look in the kitchen," he said. "With all the wires and pipes leading in, there might be a break somewhere."

Frank shrugged. "A few more minutes won't

matter, if it will make you feel better."

They went to the kitchen, where the windows and back door were locked. Frank and Joe carefully tested the pipes and wires. They were examining an electrical outlet when they detected an acrid smell.

"Gas!" Joe cried. "The tornado must have broken the pipe!"

Whirling around to warn Wilbur, Frank noticed that the butler was gone. The Hardys rushed to the door and Joe twisted the handle. The door refused to budge.

"It's locked!" he exclaimed. "Wilbur's locked us in!"

"Quick, open the window while I look for the broken pipe!" Frank commanded. "Maybe we can patch it." He got down on his hands and knees and peered under the gas stove.

Joe did as he was told, then checked the top of the stove. "Hold it, Frank!" he called out. "The stove's on, but the pilot light's out. That's why the gas is escaping!" He turned the stove off.

As Frank got to his feet, Wilbur came through the door. "I heard a noise outside so I went to see what it was, but I didn't find anything," he explained.

"Why did you lock the door?" Frank demanded.

"I didn't!" The butler looked surprised, then he examined the lock from the outside. "Oh, someone switched the lever so it locks by itself," he said. "I don't know who did it."

"You're lying!" Frank was furious. "You tricked us into coming in here and then you turned the stove on and locked us in!"

The butler's guilty look told the Hardys Frank was right, but Wilbur refused to confess.

They went out into the yard and reported to Mr. McVay that the house was sound, but that there was a lot of debris left by the tornado.

The rancher was relieved. "Perkins, you go back to the bunkhouse and supervise the cleaning operation there," he said. "The rest of you, please get busy in the house. I want it straightened out by sundown."

The Hardys pitched in to help. They were in the kitchen when they were startled by a shriek of horror in the basement.

"The Crimson Flame!" McVay bellowed. "It's gone!"

The boys raced down the stairs. The door of the vault was open. McVay stood inside, white as a sheet, holding the lid of the jewel case in his trembling right hand.

Frank and Joe rushed into the vault and saw that the place on the black velvet formerly occupied by the giant ruby was, indeed, empty!

10 Grand Canyon Caper

The Hardys at once searched the basement. Frank, inspecting the secret switch behind the stairs, discovered that the burglar alarm was turned off. Joe found the back door open and swinging on its hinges.

"Here's where the thief got in," he called out. "The door must have been unbolted because he didn't break in. He just pushed the door open and walked in!"

"And the burglar alarm was turned off," Frank added. "It must be an inside job! I suspect Wilbur!"

"So do I, Frank. Let's confront him and see if he'll talk!"

Just then the butler came down the stairs. "Is anything wrong?" he asked. "I heard Mr. Mc-Vay's voice—"

"Wilbur, we think you turned off the burglar alarm and unbolted the basement door, so your co-conspirator could get in and steal the Crimson Flame," Frank challenged him. "It all happened while the house was empty!"

Wilbur sneered. "That's ridiculous. I went outside with Mr. McVay after the tornado hit, then came back in with you boys. You know that!"

"You did it while we were searching the kitchen," Joe declared.

"You forget that the door to the vault was locked," Wilbur mocked him. "No one can unlock it without knowing the combination. And Mr. McVay is the only one who knows it."

The rancher nodded. "I never open the door except when I'm in the basement by myself. Wilbur always waits at the top of the stairs. He couldn't make out the numbers on the dial at that distance."

Wilbur grinned sardonically and the Hardys looked baffled upon hearing McVay's revelation.

"Well, it *has* to be an inside job," Joe insisted. "We'd better question the servants."

They went upstairs and Mr. McVay sent Wilbur to bring everyone to the living room. Then he called Sheriff Gomez. Through the window, Frank and Joe noticed Mr. Jomo talking to Perkins outside. When Perkins walked off, Jomo entered the house.

"The tornado missed my ranch," he said. "But I saw it headed in your direction, so I came over to see if I could be of help. Perkins just told me about the Crimson Flame. I hope the thief didn't get away!"

"He may have," Frank said grimly, and with Mr. McVay's permission, he began to interrogate the staff. All denied any knowledge of the ruby robbery. Finally Sheriff Gomez drove up with one of his deputies. After being filled in about the case, he ordered everybody to be searched. But none of the servants had the ruby!

Mr. Jomo insisted that he be included in the search. He turned his pockets inside out and allowed the sheriff to frisk him. Then he raised his hand covered by the bandage and said, "I've only got a sore under here, and no Crimson Flame. But you might as well make sure!"

Sheriff Gomez gently pressed his thumb along the gauze. "You don't have the ruby," he agreed. "Is anything else missing?"

The rancher shook his head. "The rest of the jewels are still in the vault."

"Sheriff, the thief may have hidden the gem in the house," Joe suggested, "with the intent to recover it when you're gone."

"True. We'd better search the premises," Gomez declared.

The Hardys joined the sheriff and his deputy, and Wilbur went along to guide them through the building. Every room was thoroughly inspected. In Wilbur's room, Frank noticed a pair of compact binoculars on a shelf in the closet.

"I'm an amateur bird-watcher," the butler explained. "We have marvelous birds here in Arizona. I watch them whenever I can."

The search of the house turned up nothing. By the time it was finished, night was falling. Sheriff Gomez and his deputy drove off to check on fences of stolen jewels.

McVay took the Hardys into his study and shut the door. "What can we do now?" he asked in despair.

"Well, the sheriff is watching to see if the gem turns up with a crooked dealer," Frank pointed out. "I'd like to check out the clue we have to the mysterious rider—the hat he dropped when I grabbed him. We can ask around in Flagstaff who sold it to him."

"But the mysterious rider wasn't here," McVay said, puzzled.

"Maybe he used his mirror to flash an order for the thief to take advantage of the tornado and steal the Crimson Flame," Joe observed.

McVay finally nodded. "Follow up any clues you find," he told the Hardys.

After breakfast the next morning, Frank and Joe took the ranch pickup and drove to Flagstaff. Leaving the vehicle in a parking lot, they made a tour of the stores selling hats. Most of the merchants they showed the hat to were baffled by it. But one, who ran a hatter's establishment near Arizona State College, recognized it.

"This comes from the Far East," he said. "I've seen the type on my trips to Hong Kong." He peered at the label. "This explains it. The letters B-A-N-G stand for Bangkok, Thailand. That's where the hat was manufactured. But I think you'll have to go to Bangkok to find out more, because no American importer handles this make. By the way, where did you get it?"

"I picked it up in the desert," Frank replied. "Somebody dropped it there."

The Hardys left the store and stopped on a street corner to decide what to do next. Suddenly a familiar voice greeted them: "Howdy, pardners!"

The brothers whirled around and saw a chubby boy in a gaudy Western outfit. He was wearing a ten-gallon hat, a plaid shirt with a polka dot neckerchief, corduroy trousers with leather chaps, and cowboy boots. His thumbs were hooked in his belt.

"Chet!" Frank burst out. "We certainly didn't expect to see you here!"

Biff Hooper, who was dressed in ordinary ranch working clothes, stood behind his friend and chuckled. "He's a real cowhand now. In charge of the chuck wagon. I'm helping the blacksmith. You sure found us good jobs in Arizona."

The four Bayport youths went to a small restaurant, where they ordered hamburgers and sodas. Chet and Biff took turns describing how they had flown to Arizona and started working at once at Jake Jomo's ranch. This was their free day so they had driven into Flagstaff.

"You're supposed to catch the rustlers, not take time off," Joe needled his friends.

"There hasn't been any sign of rustlers," Biff said, "and Mr. Jomo told us to go into town. Everybody does, and if we had stayed at the ranch, the others would have wondered."

"How about you guys?" Chet asked. "Have you found any clues yet?"

"We're suspicious of our foreman, Wat Perkins," Joe replied.

"He was over at the Jomo ranch yesterday," Chet exclaimed.

"What was he doing there?" Joe inquired.

"I'm not sure," Chet replied. "I had gone to the storehouse to get supplies, when I realized I forgot my list. So I went back for it, and found a strange cowboy in the bunkhouse talking on the phone. I heard him say he was Wat Perkins."

"What else did he say?" Frank asked.

"He mentioned a name. Something like G. C. T. Morrow."

The Hardys looked blank. "Could that be a cowboy at the Jomo Ranch?" Joe suggested.

Biff shook his head. "No, we don't have a G. C. T. Morrow. He must be one of Mr. McVay's hands."

"He isn't with us, either," Frank said. "Did Perkins say any more?"

"No, he hung up and left the bunkhouse. His horse was in the woods in back. I saw him ride away, but he didn't see me."

"Maybe Morrow's a rustler!" Joe interjected. "He and Perkins could be planning to steal Mr. Jomo's cattle. That's why Perkins sneaked into the bunkhouse when nobody was there."

"But why would he go to the ranch where he's planning to rustle cattle?" Frank objected. "He'd make the call from somewhere else. That name G. C. T. Morrow seems phony to me. Who uses three initials out here?"

Joe had an idea. "G. C. could stand for Grand Canyon. Perhaps Perkins was saying that he'd meet somebody at the Grand Canyon tomorrow! Since he said it yesterday, that means today! Let's go there and see who it is!"

The other three agreed it was worth checking out, so they paid their bill and piled into the McVay pickup. After the long drive to the Grand Canyon, they parked and went into the Visitors Center. Suddenly, in the crowd, they saw a tall man with black hair.

"It's Oscar Tamm!" Joe gasped.

The four boys filtered through the people excitedly and followed the jewel thief, who went through the exit and left the building. Splitting up so as not to be noticed, and concealing themselves among the spectators, the young detectives trailed Tamm to an area of sagebrush, pinion pines, and juniper trees. They reached an isolated spot where the terrain was dry and rough, marked by buttes and gulches.

The boys could see the panorama of the Grand Canyon between the south rim and the north rim, twelves miles across and stretching out of sight to the east and the west. Massive escarpments undulated through the chasms. Rock strata, millions of years old, fell sharply down the sides in a multicolored display of limestone, sandstone, and granite. A mile below, the Colorado River flowed along the floor of the canyon, which it had created through erosion over eons.

The boys had no time to revel in the spectacle, however. They followed Tamm until he disappeared around a small butte.

Just before they reached it, Frank stopped short and held his hand up. "Sh!" he whispered. "I hear voices!"

After a few moments, he crept up to where he could look around the butte from the protective cover of small juniper trees. Then he motioned for the others to follow him.

Joe had to stifle a gasp when he saw Tamm talking to Wat Perkins! A third man stood listening to them. He was medium-sized, with sleek brown hair and steel-rimmed spectacles.

"The ruby's your responsibility," Perkins was saying to Tamm.

"No problem, as long as the Hardys don't butt in," Tamm growled.

The third man spoke in a scoffing manner. "I

can take care of them or my name ain't Nick Summers. They'll never recognize me after the disguise I wore in New York when I tailed them in the green compact. And they can't get to me through the car since I stole it for the job and abandoned it in Central Park."

Tamm grinned evilly. "That was a good job Nick pulled off," he told Perkins. "When I didn't come out of the subway where he was waiting, he decided to tail McVay."

"I figured he got away," Summers declared, "and that you'd go to McVay's hotel. So I went there and parked."

"We worked out a great scheme," Tamm said. "Nick phoned McVay and kept him on the line while I climbed through the window from the fire escape. I'd have grabbed the Crimson Flame right then except for the Hardys. How could I know they'd be with McVay?"

"They seem to turn up everywhere," Perkins grumbled. "But I bet they won't follow you to Bangkok!"

11   *Flight to Adventure*

The four boys stared at one another. They strained their ears to hear what Perkins would say next.

"I have to get back to the ranch before McVay starts to wonder," the foreman went on. "What bugs me is that the Hardys are already suspicious of me. They know that I ran the pickup at them on the drive from the airport to the ranch, and that I put the burr under Joe's saddle. They're also aware that I told Marti to leave the corral gate open so they'd chase the bronc while I was getting signals from the boss."

"That's too bad, but we can't help it," Tamm said. "Let's take the pledge and then split."

The three men joined hands, chanting in unison: "Power to the Blue Triangle! Power to the Blue Triangle!"

Just then a gust of wind blew dust into Chet's face. He felt his eyes water and his nose itch. Desperately, he placed a finger against his upper lip. Too late! He caught his breath and let out a terrific sneeze!

The three men started at the sound. Realizing that there was no point in hiding any longer, Frank, Joe, and Biff jumped up and rushed away.

"Someone's eavesdropping on us!" Tamm shouted. "Let's get out of here!" With that, he, Perkins, and Summers ran down from the butte and along the cliff.

The boys were some distance behind the fleeing men when Biff suddenly slipped at the edge of the cliff where the drop was straight down the Grand Canyon to the Colorado River!

Frank was close enough to make a flying leap and grab his friend by the arm just as he was going over the precipice. Bracing his foot against a pinion pine sapling, he held on until Joe raced up and took Biff by the other arm. Together, the Hardys hauled their friend back to safety.

"Thanks a lot," Biff gulped. "A cramp made my leg give way. But I'm okay now. Let's go!"

"Where's Chet?" Joe asked.

The boys looked around, but saw no sign of their chubby buddy. Hastily, they retraced their steps until a remarkable sight met their eyes. Chet was lodged in a crevice between two rocks, wedged in so tightly that he could not get out by himself!

Plaintively he looked up at them. "I thought you were going to leave me here! How about giving me a hand?"

In spite of their sympathy, Biff and the Hardys could not help but laugh at Chet's woebegone appearance.

"Maybe we *will* leave you there until you get thinner and can make it by yourself!" Biff needled.

"That is *not* funny!" Chet protested.

"Calm down, we'll bring you water!" Biff went on.

"What if Perkins and his gang find me?"

"Aw, he's right, Biff," Joe said. "We'd better pull him out." He and Frank leaned in, took Chet by the hands, and used a lot of leverage to lift him free of the rocks.

"Are you hurt?" Frank asked anxiously.

"No, except for a skinned knee and a bruised elbow. I'll live."

The foursome walked to the parking lot, got into the pickup, and began the drive back to

Flagstaff. Along the way they discussed the strange things that they had witnessed at the Grand Canyon.

"What are Tamm and Summers doing in Arizona?" Chet wondered.

"I bet they were told to come here by the boss, who must be the same person who informed them about Mr. McVay being in New York," Frank said. "No doubt they stole the Crimson Flame!"

"And then there's Bangkok," Joe put in. "That's where the hat came from, and that's where Tamm is going!"

"Maybe to sell the gem," Chet ventured.

Biff scratched his head. "Do you have any idea what the Blue Triangle is?"

"Suppose it's a cattle brand!" Chet exclaimed. "I'll check the ranches around here and see if one of them uses a blue triangle to brand its longhorns!"

Frank was doubtful. "But why would they be chanting like that if that were the case?" he asked.

None of the boys had an answer, and they continued on in silence.

Once they reached Flagstaff, Biff and Chet drove to the Jomo ranch, while the Hardys returned to the McVay ranch in the pickup.

They found the rancher in great distress.

"Perkins has disappeared!" McVay shouted when he saw them. "He took one of the cars and drove off last night. He hasn't been seen since!"

"That figures," Joe declared. "Perkins may have stolen the Crimson Flame. He's mixed up with Oscar Tamm and Nick Summers."

"But Tamm and Summers are in New York! You saw them there!"

"Now they're here. They were meeting with Perkins."

Frank told what had happened at the Grand Canyon. "We heard Perkins say that the ruby is Tamm's responsibility. After that, he mentioned that Tamm was going to Bangkok, where the hat came from that the mysterious rider dropped. We think he may try to sell the Crimson Flame when he gets there."

The rancher became impassioned. "That's it, Frank! My ruby has great resale value on the black market in Bangkok. Many dishonest collectors buy their jewels there."

Just then Sheriff Gomez arrived. "There's no break in the Crimson Flame case," he said glumly. "Have you boys discovered any clues?"

Frank nodded. "We were just about to call you, sheriff." He quickly explained about Perkins, Tamm, and Summers.

"I'll put out an all-points bulletin," Sheriff

Gomez promised. "All airports will be watched. What are you boys going to do next?"

"I think they should go to Bangkok in case Tamm gets away," McVay said.

"Good idea," Gomez agreed. "Now, I'll phone headquarters and have that bulletin issued."

When he returned after making his call, Joe said, "Have you ever heard of a Blue Triangle?"

Both men looked at him, puzzled.

"Not me," McVay replied, and the sheriff shrugged.

"Our friend, Biff Hooper, thinks it may be a cattle brand," Frank spoke up.

The sheriff shook his head. "I know all the brands in the Arizona ranchman's almanac. No one uses a blue triangle to identify his cattle."

A few minutes later, Sheriff Gomez left and McVay turned to the Hardys. "I have more than one reason to send you to Bangkok. My agent there reported another giant ruby has been found at the mines of To Kor, and I'd like to have it for my collection. You boys can kill two birds with one stone—search for Tamm and the Crimson Flame, and buy the new ruby for me. I authorize you to pay fifty thousand dollars for it."

"We can kill a third bird," Frank said, withdrawing the mysterious rider's hat from his pocket. "We'll try to find out who bought this."

"You're willing to go, then?" McVay inquired eagerly.

Joe nodded. "We'll have to check with Dad, though."

"Who's your agent? And where can we find him?" Frank asked.

"His name is Bo Dai. He's at the Thieves Market in Bangkok."

"The Thieves Market?" Frank and Joe exclaimed together.

The rancher chuckled. "It's an old name. Goes back to the time when thieves had a stranglehold on the market. Things have changed since then. Not that you boys shouldn't be careful when you get there. The Thieves Market isn't entirely free of criminals! Be careful, especially if you get the second ruby. Incidentally, you won't need visas for Thailand if you don't stay more than fifteen days."

Frank grinned. "I hope it won't take us that long!"

McVay opened a desk drawer and lifted out a small yellow stone, which he handed to Frank. "This is a topaz, not very valuable, but don't lose it. When you get to Bangkok, show it to Bo

Dai. It will identify you to him as my representatives."

The three discussed details of the trip. The Hardys agreed to catch a plane to Los Angeles the following day and fly from there to Bangkok. They made the travel arrangements over the phone and talked to their father, who agreed to the plan.

After that, Frank and Joe called the bunkhouse at the Jomo ranch to inform Chet and Biff of their new plans.

"Boy, I wish we could come along," Chet said. "There's no sign of rustlers around here so far and life isn't very exciting at all!"

"You wanted a summer job, didn't you?" Frank said.

"I know, I know. But I'd rather go to Thailand any day!"

"Don't worry, we'll stay on the case at this end," Biff put in. "And we'll report to Sheriff Gomez if we find out anything."

The next evening Frank and Joe were airborne on the plane from Flagstaff to Los Angeles. They transferred to a jumbo jet, which thundered over the Pacific. After touching down in Hawaii, they took out the literature the airline provided on Thailand.

Joe traced the site of Bangkok on the map.

"It's on the Gulf of Thailand," he noted. "The Chao Phraya River runs through it. And there are so many canals, they call Bangkok the Venice of Thailand."

Frank was reading up on the archeology of the country. "There are temples in the jungle almost as important as those of Angkor Wat, the ancient temple ruins in the Cambodian jungle," he said. "Many are in the process of being restored."

After a while, Joe replaced his pamphlet in its holder and gazed out of the window, where white clouds were drifting along far below their jet.

"Frank, I'm beginning to wonder if McVay is leveling with us," he said. "Suppose he's stolen his own ruby for the insurance and is sending us on a wild-goose chase to get us out of the way?"

12 The Thieves Market

Frank stared at his brother for a moment, then slowly shook his head. "I doubt it," he said. "Tamm's attack on McVay in New York looked like the real thing to me. If McVay was in cahoots with the thief, he could simply have handed him the ruby."

"I suppose so," Joe said. "Well, we have a long trip ahead of us. I think I'll take a snooze." He leaned back in his seat and closed his eyes. Frank did the same, and they soon were fast asleep.

When they awoke, the plane was landing at Don Muang Airport near Bangkok.

Yawning and stretching, the Hardys filed off

the craft with the rest of the passengers. They presented their passports for inspection at the gate, gathered their baggage, and went to the airport hotel. The staff spoke English, so the two Americans had no trouble checking in.

They had been in their room for only a few minutes when the phone rang. "Who could that be?" Frank wondered. "Not many people know we're here."

"Maybe the desk clerk wanting to sell us a guided tour of the city," Joe said. He picked up the phone. A voice spoke in English with a distinct Thai accent. "Hardys, I know why you're here! The next plane for America leaves in one hour. Be on it! This is your only warning!"

There was a click and the line went dead. Joe replaced the receiver in its cradle and relayed to Frank what he had heard.

"Someone's trying to scare us off!" Frank muttered. "But how does he know we're here?"

"We need some answers, that's for sure," Joe said. "Let's see if we can find them at the Thieves Market."

They went out of the hotel and took a taxi to Bangkok. The city was a combination of old and new. The crowds in the streets wore both Oriental and Western dress. Motorboats raced by, splashing spray on sampans riding on the river and the canals. Buddhist temples faced modern high-rise apartments.

The taxi turned onto Maha Chai Road, and soon the driver pulled to a stop at the Thieves Market. Since he spoke a little English, the boys asked him if he could tell them where to find Bo Dai.

"The middle of the market," the man said and gave them directions.

"Thank you," Frank said and the young detectives walked into a colorful, noisy throng moving back and forth in the streets. Stall owners hawked their wares in cajoling voices, tempting passersby to purchase antiques, souvenirs, furniture, clothing, and food.

Suddenly Joe noticed a man following them. He was a Thai dressed in a brown shirt, khaki shorts, and heavy boots. In his belt he wore a dagger.

"We've got a shadow!" Joe warned in an urgent undertone.

Pretending to be interested in a flower stall, Frank paused, turned his head, and glanced out of the corner of his eye. "I see him too. Let's use our shadow technique on him."

By "shadow technique" Frank meant a system he and Joe had worked out for dealing with crooks who were spying on them. They always

pretended not to be aware they were being followed until they could ambush the spy.

The Hardys strolled through the crowd, looking nonchalantly from side to side as if they
were ordinary American tourists. By stopping at
an occasional stall, they were able to glance
back and see their pursuer. When they stopped,
he stopped. When they moved on, he moved
on. At last they turned a corner to the rear of a
line of stalls. Joe ducked behind an oblong
teakwood post projecting from one stall. Frank
walked on by himself.

Peering through a crack between the post and
the stall, Joe saw the Thai turn the corner and
go after Frank. When he passed the teakwood
post, the Hardy boy stepped out, trapping the
man between himself and his brother.

Frank, who had listened to the footsteps following him, suddenly whirled around.

The man stared at him, then turned back.
When he saw Joe, he reached for his dagger!

Without hesitating, Joe piled into him, bowling him over and knocking the dagger from his
hand. It fell to the ground, where Frank picked
it up. Then they pulled the man to his feet.

"Who are you and why are you following
us?" Joe demanded.

The Thai let out a flood of words, shook his

head and extended his palm as if to say he did not understand. The owner of the stall, hearing the scuffle, came out the back door. He spoke English and offered to help.

"Ask this man who he is," Frank appealed to him.

The two men conversed in Thai. "His name is Teng Prasit," the stall owner finally offered. "He does not know English."

"Why is he following us?"

The two men talked in Thai again. Teng Prasit smiled, shook his head, and spoke emphatically. "He says he realized you were American tourists, and he followed you because he thought you might want to buy his dagger," the interpreter said.

The Hardys realized there was no charge they could make against Teng Prasit with the police, so Frank handed him the dagger. "No thanks, we're not interested," he said shortly.

Teng Prasit smiled again. He brandished the dagger in a wide arc that made Joe jump out of the way to avoid its point. Then he walked back into the Thieves Market and disappeared. The Hardys thanked their interpreter and went looking for Bo Dai until they saw the sign: BO DAI, RUBY AGENT.

114

They entered the stall and found a plump, brown man who greeted them with an engaging smile. "I see you are Americans," he said. "What can I do for you?"

"Are you Bo Dai?" Frank inquired.

"I am."

Frank took McVay's yellow topaz from his pocket and handed it to Bo Dai, who examined it carefully before giving it back.

"So, you are from Mr. McVay. I assume you have come about the second giant ruby, which I reported to him was recently found at To Kor."

"Mr. McVay commissioned us to buy it," Joe informed the agent.

Bo Dai nodded. "I will take you to the mines. We can depart this evening if you will return at that time."

"We'll be here," Joe assured him.

"Incidentally, you are not the only Americans interested in the To Kor ruby," Bo Dai continued. "Two others came here to inquire about it only a few hours ago."

"Who are they?" Frank burst out. "Do you know their names?"

The ruby agent nodded. "Oscar Tamm and Nick Summers."

115

The news made Joe gasp, and Frank felt his nerves tingle.

"Tamm and Summers are crooks!" Joe exploded. "They'll steal the ruby if you let them!"

Bo Dai rubbed his palms together. "I had a feeling that they were not honest from the way they conducted themselves, so I told them nothing about the To Kor ruby. But there are other agents here who will cooperate with them."

Frank saw the point. "We'd better get to the mine before Tamm and Summers do. If we can corner them there, we may even recover the Crimson Flame."

The Hardys described the theft at McVay's ranch. Bo Dai shook his head sadly. "That is a great misfortune," he said. "Well, I am prepared to close my stall at sunset, and we will leave for To Kor."

Frank and Joe decided to use the time to search for the seller of the mysterious hat. They went from one hat stall to another until they came to a dealer who recognized it. He spoke to them through an interpreter.

"I designed this hat for an American who wanted an unusually broad brim," he recalled. "He bought two of them. I do not know his

116

name, but he wore a long beard and a mustache."

Joe felt disappointed. "He was disguised! There's no way of telling who he was."

The hatter shrugged. "There was one more thing about him."

"What's that?" Frank inquired.

"He has a blue triangle tattooed on the back of his right hand."

"That figures," Joe said as they went out into the crowd again. "Maybe he's the boss of the gang."

"Tamm or Summers could have blue triangles on their hands," Frank said.

Joe nodded. "Maybe. Hey, let's get some chow. I'm starved."

The two walked to a food stand, and were eating an exotic rice dish with chopsticks when suddenly they froze.

Oscar Tamm was looking at them from the middle of the crowd in front of them!

When he realized that the Hardys had seen him, he moved rapidly away, heading for a souvenir stall on the other side. Frank and Joe abandoned their half-eaten meal and dashed after him. Seeing him go into the stall, they ran up and entered the establishment. It was filled with imitation jewelry, plaster statuettes, flags,

117

posters, postcards, and other cheap items. The front room was empty, so the Hardys walked through to the back.

Tamm was just disappearing out the rear door. Frank and Joe bounded forward to give chase. They were in the middle of the room when Summers stepped from behind a large, ornamental war flag draped from a crossbar overhead. Smirking at them, he took hold of a cord dangling from the ceiling and jerked it!

A trapdoor fell open beneath their feet and Frank and Joe plummeted into the dark basement! Then the door closed over their heads!

13   The Mines of To Kor

The Hardys landed with a thump on a wooden floor, and the impact dazed them for a moment.

"Joe, can you see anything?" Frank inquired when his head cleared.

"I'm seeing stars!" Joe confessed ruefully. "Where are we?"

"I don't know."

When their eyes became accustomed to the gloom, they realized they were in a small room entirely surrounded by stone walls. There was no door, and no sound came from the room overhead.

"The only way out is through the trapdoor," Frank said thoughtfully. "And that's so high, they may figure we can't reach it. Perhaps they left it open!"

Joe rubbed his aching head. "So who climbs up?"

"Be my guest," Frank said and braced his hands on his knees. Joe climbed onto his brother's shoulders, and when Frank straightened up, Joe rose to his feet. Precariously balanced, he felt for the trapdoor.

"Hurry up!" Frank grated. "I'll go through the floor in a minute!"

Joe checked the door, then leaped down.

"It's locked," he said. "We're caught!"

Desperately, Frank stared around the room. Noticing a brick lying in one corner, he walked over and ran his hands over the wall. Several other bricks were loose. Excitedly he called to Joe, and the two of them began pulling bricks from the wall and setting them on the floor.

When the opening was big enough, Frank poked his head in. "It's pitch dark," he whispered over his shoulder, "but it's the only way for us to go. Follow me!"

He crawled through on his hands and knees, and kept going until he ran into a barrier made up of vertical bamboo bars. "We can't go any farther," he told Joe, who was right behind him. "This bamboo is the heaviest I've ever touched.

An elephant couldn't break through this."

Suddenly there was a slithering sound, and a loud thump in back of them. Turning around, Joe hit a similar bamboo barrier. A light flashed on, forcing the boys to cover their eyes, which by now were accustomed to the darkness. When they were able to stand the light and drop their hands, they saw they were in a cage made of broad bamboo rods fitted into sockets at the top and the bottom on all four sides. The slithering sound and the thump had been made by a sliding door falling into place behind them.

"We're caught in a tiger trap!" Frank exploded. "We crawled right into it!"

They heard Tamm's voice from the other side of the trap. "That was our plan, and you fell for it. The Hardys aren't such great detectives after all!"

"We had to take our chances," Joe grumbled. "Anyway, this ball game isn't over yet."

"Oh, yes, it is! You just made the last play—or should I say error!" Tamm scoffed at him. "I spotted you in the hotel lobby, then had a friend phone you. He warned you to leave Thailand, but you didn't listen. So I lured you into this little trap and now you'll stay—permanently!"

Summers walked up. "Everything's ready,"

he said to Tamm. "The truck will be here in a few minutes."

The two thieves went around to the sliding door of the tiger trap.

Summers took a strong leather strap from his pocket and handed it to Tamm, who fastened the door shut and tied the ends of the strap into a sailor's knot. The Hardys noted that neither of the men had a blue triangle tattooed on the back of his right hand.

Just then a truck drove up to the open door and the driver leaped out of the cab. *He was Teng Prasit!*

"I am ready for the drive to the Gulf of Thailand!" he called out.

"So you do speak English!" Frank exclaimed. "You're the one who phoned that warning message to the airport hotel. Now I recognize your voice!"

"And that was pure nonsense about selling us your dagger!" Joe accused him.

Teng Prasit grinned. "You are both correct. Our plan was for me to finish you off with my dagger if I could. I admit you were too quick for me. But you were not too quick for the tiger trap!"

Tamm became impatient. "Nick and I've got to hit the road," he urged. "Teng Prasit, you stay in the truck till dark. Then somebody'll come and help you load the trap. Take it to the Gulf and dump it in."

Tamm snapped off the light, and the three went out, closing the door behind them. Silence fell over the dark room where the Hardys were caged in the tiger trap.

Joe turned around on his hands and knees. He felt between the bamboo bars of the sliding door to see if he could untie the knot. His fingertips barely brushed it.

"No way I can get this loose," he declared. "I'll have to try cutting it."

He took his detective kit from his pocket and selected a long, thin blade that was razor-sharp. Easing up beside him in the narrow confines of the trap, Frank produced his pencil flashlight. Then, while Frank kept the beam fixed on the leather strap, Joe pushed his blade between the bars, maneuvered the cutting edge onto the knot, and began to saw back and forth.

"We've got to get out of here before they come for us!" he said anxiously, pausing to flex his fingers to relieve the strain.

"Keep going. You're almost through," Frank encouraged him.

Joe resumed wielding his blade. Finally the knot snapped apart as the miniature knife bit through the final strands, and the leather strap fell to the floor. Gingerly, Joe pushed up the sliding door and climbed out of the tiger trap. He held the gate up while Frank followed, and then moved it back into place without making a sound.

The boys put their detective tools away and stole across the room to the door, which Frank opened a crack. They were able to see Teng Prasit in the cab of the truck. He was slouched down in the seat with his head tilted back, his eyes closed and his mouth open.

Lucky for us he's asleep, Frank thought. He gestured to Joe with his head and both slipped outside. Sneaking past the truck, they hurried to Bo Dai's stall. When the gem agent heard their story, he at once alerted a patrolling policeman, who promised to arrest Teng Prasit and search for Tamm and Summers.

"They may be headed for To Kor," Joe pointed out. "We heard Tamm say something about hitting the road. That's where they'll go if they're after the ruby."

"We will radio a warning to the police in the To Kor area," the officer promised.

"I am going there tonight with the American boys," Bo Dai spoke up. "We will look for the thieves ourselves."

They piled into his car and he drove across Bangkok. Beyond the city they took an old road leading to the southeast. Gradually the traffic vanished, as they passed through the jungle where the howling of monkeys and the screeching of birds in the trees told them that nighttime predators were on the prowl.

Around midnight, Bo Dai drove into a cleared spot in the jungle provided by the government as a resting place for travelers. "Time for dinner," he announced, and they got out of the car. He produced some dried fish and bamboo shoots, which they consumed sitting on a teak log. Finally Bo Dai topped off the meal by brewing a pot of tea.

Twenty minutes later, the group continued their drive, arriving at To Kor just after daybreak.

The place reminded the Hardys of a Gold Rush boom town in the American West. Shacks had sprung up in a sprawling area between the jungle and a sluggish stream. The earth was torn up where hundreds of miners had wielded their spades in the hope of striking it rich. A number had placed sluice boxes at the bottom of a cliff, against which they were spraying jets of water from large hoses. The water carried earth from the cliff into the sluices, where the rubies were stopped by slats across the boxes while the lighter debris flowed out with the water at the lower end. Other prospectors were panning the stream or pawing through gravel on its banks.

Frank glanced at the people. "They look like a tough bunch," he said.

"They are," Bo Dai confirmed. "And they protect their claims no matter what." He pointed to a large building that had heavy metal bars over the doors and windows.

"That is the ruby exchange," he said. "Here the miners sell their gems or leave them for safekeeping."

"Where do we find the guy who has the giant ruby?" Frank asked.

"Over there." Bo Dai led the way to a shack on a patch of land near the jungle that had been dug up so much it looked like a closeup of the moon. The owner was a man named Chao Mai. He was much taller than the average Thai and had a bold expression on his face.

He asked the group inside and they stood near the open door while he was talking to Bo Dai in their native language. Then the gem dealer introduced Frank and Joe and explained why they were there.

The miner smiled, reached into his pocket,

and with great pride produced a ruby about the size of the Crimson Flame. He held it between his thumb and forefinger, to let the sunlight fall on it. The gem glowed a deep crimson. Light seemed to be imprisoned within it and struggling to get out!

"It's gorgeous," Joe breathed in awe.

Suddenly, without any warning, Oscar Tamm burst through the door, violently shoving Chao Mai against the rest of the group, and at the same time snatching the ruby from his hand. As the miner, Bo Dai, and the Hardys crashed to the floor, the thief dashed out the door again and plunged into the jungle!

14   Jungle Chase

Bo Dai and Chao Mai were thunderstruck. Slowly they got up, their mouths open, and stared in bewilderment after the intruder.

Joe and Frank were already on their feet and rushing out the door. They sped across the churned-up terrain where the giant ruby and so many others had been found. Slipping and sliding in the dust and mud, they reached the edge of the jungle. By now the jewel thief was out of sight.

"Which way did he go?" Frank panted.

"Over there, I think," Joe replied, pointing to the northeast where they could hear the breaking of branches and snapping of twigs, as Tamm forced his way through the tangle of vegetation.

They plunged into the trees, vines, and undergrowth, moving as rapidly as possible in the direction of the noise, but it grew fainter and finally died away.

"He must have reached an open spot!" Joe lamented.

Frank shrugged. "We'll go where we last heard him and see if we can pick up his trail."

They hurried on and came to a clearing where Tamm had been able to move noiselessly over a carpet of thick grass. Crossing to the other side, the Hardys used their backwoods training to find where the fugitive had reentered the heavy vegetation.

Frank pointed to a broken branch dangling from a tree. "The sap is fresh," he noted. "Tamm went that way!"

They continued at a fast pace, discovering brambles holding pieces of torn cloth from Tamm's jacket. At one point, in a low-lying area softened by jungle rain, they saw the trail of his footprints across the soggy terrain, and followed until they ended on higher, dryer ground.

"He's probably still going northeast," Frank said. "Let's take a reading." He removed a small compass from his detective kit and turned it until the needle pointed to NE on the face of the dial.

Then the boys pushed on for a long stretch

without any sign of the fugitive.

"The brambles are spaced too widely here to catch on Tamm's jacket," Frank said in frustration. "And the ground is too dry for footprints. We can't tell which way he went."

"I'll climb a tree," Joe suggested. "Maybe I can spot him." Selecting the tallest tree, the younger Hardy took hold of a low branch and swung himself up. He climbed higher amid leaves and creepers, until he reached a point where he could see far over the smaller trees to an open glade. Tamm was just hurrying to the other side.

"There he is!" Joe called out in excitement. "He's still headed in the same direction!"

Suddenly, there was a rustling in the foliage above his head. What at first looked like a thick creeper draped over a branch began to move toward him. A snout poked through the leaves followed by a triangular head, and a pair of cold reptilian eyes glared at them as a long, sinuous body moved along the branch.

Joe did not wait to see more. He dropped to the branch below and slid down the tree, until he tumbled to the ground.

"What's the big hurry?" his brother teased. "You got a date?"

"Oh, no," Joe said casually. "Just a python. Let's get out of here!"

Frank took one look at the reptile and turned instantly on his heels. "Eeeech!" he yelled. "Let's!"

By the time they reached the open glade, Tamm was gone, but they found a narrow trail used apparently by Thai hunters. Newly depressed blades of grass revealed that the thief had passed that way only minutes ago. They followed the trail until they heard the gurgling of shallow water over stones, and crossed a broad stream by jumping from one rock to another.

The trail turned to the west on the other side, but the bent grass proved to their trained eyes that Tamm had stayed on his course to the northeast. They entered a gloomy region of the jungle where the tops of the trees blocked out the sky. Colorful birds fluttered their wings on the branches and cawed at the Hardys. Monkeys scampered from treetop to treetop, as snakes and scorpions slithered out of the way. Blue orchids growing profusely amid the bushes gave off a strong perfume that drifted on the wind.

"This is a spooky place!" Joe muttered, as the glade gave way to a bamboo thicket. Suddenly they heard sounds coming directly toward them!

Frank pulled Joe to one side behind a bush.

"If that's Tamm, he has a gang with him!" he whispered.

The noise came nearer. Tall bamboo shoots bent forward and lay flattened on the ground. An elephant came through and plodded on into another part of the jungle. Three smaller ones followed in single file.

"That's a gang I'd like to have!" Joe chuckled. "Nobody would fool with us!"

Frank grinned. "What an offensive line for our football team! We'd make a first down on every play!"

They came to some hills where a pass divided two steep cliffs. Joe spotted a large black button in the middle of the pass and picked it up.

"This is from Tamm's jacket," he judged. "I recognize it. He went through this pass."

A sudden snarl made their blood freeze. Looking up, they saw a tiger poised on the top of one cliff! It snarled again and sprang at them!

On a reflex action, the Hardys hit the ground. The big cat flew over them, crashed into the rocky wall of the opposite cliff, and fell to the ground. It lay there stunned by the impact.

Frank and Joe lost no time scrambling through the pass. They ran as fast and as far as they could. At last they stopped to catch their breath.

"I thought there were no man-eating tigers in Thailand!" Frank panted, leaning over with his hands on his knees.

"This one must have missed his dinner last night," Joe quipped. "When he spotted us, he figured we'd make a good meal. Hardy hamburger!"

Breathing more easily, they went forward until night fell over the jungle. Realizing they could not follow Tamm's trail in the darkness, they found refuge under an arching bush, made a meal of fruit and berries, and went to sleep. The rising sun woke them. After a quick breakfast, they continued on their trek, which eventually brought them to another trail. There they were able to follow Tamm's footprints in the dust.

"We're getting close," Frank warned after a while. "These prints are so new the dirt hasn't covered them yet."

The boys moved cautiously forward, pausing occasionally to listen for suspicious sounds. Finally the trail led into a walk paved with flat stones.

"It must lead somewhere," Joe commented. "But I don't hear a sound up ahead."

They continued through the jungle on one side of the walk, and came to a point where they could see an open area through the trees. They dropped to the ground and crawled behind a cluster of giant ferns. Pushing the fronds apart, the Hardys gasped in surprise!

The walk led up to an opening in a stone wall that extended on both sides and curved backward in a circle. Beyond the wall, the walk continued across a bare area to a huge temple. It was a tall structure, made of enormous stone blocks, and ringed at the top by carved stone figures. There were paneless windows in its sides at every level.

"Wow!" Joe breathed. "An ancient temple in the middle of nowhere!"

A rat bounded across the stone walk, and a hawk dropped out of the sky, zoomed down, grabbed it in its talons, and flew off.

Frank nudged Joe. "Come on. Maybe Tamm's hiding in these ruins. If he went on past, we'll have to pick up his trail again."

Joe nodded. "Let's scout around the wall. I'll go left, you'll go right. We'll meet behind the temple and compare notes." He moved away along the wall, clambered over moss-covered stone blocks, and pushed his way through vines climbing on top of the barrier enclosing the compound. Every dozen yards or so he stopped to reconnoiter, scanning the temple for suspicious movements and listening for sounds that might call for investigation.

Finally he saw Frank approaching from the opposite direction. Neither boy had encountered anything suspicious.

"But that doesn't prove anything," Frank pointed out. "Tamm may be hiding in the temple. We'll have to take a chance and go in!"

15 Temple Trap

The Hardys moved cautiously along the walk and through the doorway. Inside, they saw stone statues badly eroded by time and the weather. The faces had long, vertical lines where rain had poured down them over the centuries.

"They look like they're crying," Joe commented.

Frank chuckled. "They're sad because it's the rainy season. Actually, we're lucky that the weather has held up the last couple of days. We've caught a break in the monsoon, but we'll probably get drenched any minute."

"Please," Joe said. "We have enough troubles."

They mounted the temple staircase to a platform from which arose the upper stories. The main doorway admitted them to a large, square room. Stone benches ran around the walls, and a raised dais at the far end held a massive stone chair with a high back.

Frank felt an eerie sensation as he gazed around. "This must have been the throne room," he muttered.

Joe nodded. "It looks as if no one has been here for centuries."

They walked across the room to a staircase behind the throne that led them to the second story. There a number of smaller rooms were completely empty, except for one, where the Hardys saw three rusty swords lying in a corner.

Joe picked one up, testing the point with his thumb. "It's still sharp," he noted.

Frank nodded. "I guess we're in the arsenal where—" He broke off because he heard a sound overhead. He gestured to Joe and they stood breathlessly, without moving a muscle. The sound was repeated several times, a scuffling noise approaching the head of the stairs.

"Somebody's coming down!" Joe whispered hoarsely. "Could be Tamm!"

Frank nodded, placing a finger over his lips at the same time. He jerked his head toward the stairs, and they quickly tiptoed over to the doorway. There they flattened themselves against the wall on either side, prepared to leap on Tamm as he came through the doorway.

The sounds overhead reached the top of the stairs, then a spherical brown object bounced down the steps and through the doorway into the room.

Joe stared at it bug-eyed. "It's a coconut!" He gulped.

The boys peered up the stairs and saw a monkey grinning at them. They burst into laughter. Startled by the sound, the monkey scampered away. Frank and Joe quickly went up the stairs and saw how monkeys could get into the room from a coconut tree beside it.

The brothers continued through the building until they came out on the turret at the top, which was enclosed by a low stone parapet. Jungle vines extended their tentacles over it after having climbed up the exterior walls.

Joe looked around. "It's an interesting place, but we've lost Tamm's trail. What do we do now?"

Frank shielded his eyes with his hand and turned around, scanning the jungle in every direction. "We just picked up the trail again!" he exclaimed. "Look over there!"

Joe turned and saw that a number of men were emerging from the jungle in single file and heading for the doorway to the temple. Tamm was in the lead, with Summers right behind him. The rest were sinister-looking Thais. They entered and made their way up the central staircase into the temple, crossed the throne room, then started up the stairs.

"Frank, if they come all the way, we're trapped!" Joe whispered. "The stairs are the only way down!"

Frank looked grim as he whispered back, "Get ready for action! Maybe we can grab Tamm and make the others back off!"

But the men stopped at the landing just below the turret, and entered one of the rooms. Tamm was speaking to the Thais in their own language, then switched to English when he addressed Summers.

"I've been here lots of times," he said. "It's like fairyland with all those rubies around!"

"But you didn't get the Crimson Flame last time you were here," Summers observed.

"I came to Bangkok as soon as I heard about it," Tamm defended himself. "Trouble was, Bo Dai had shipped it to the States the day before I arrived. So I hustled back to New York and almost got it from McVay, except those Hardy boys interfered."

"Too bad they got away from Teng Prasit,"

Summers grumbled. "Otherwise they'd be in the Gulf of Thailand by now."

Tamm mumbled something and finished with, "Anyway, the Blue Triangle has the Crimson Flame."

"Neat thing, that blue triangle," Summers observed. "The Thais think it has occult power, so they obey anyone who shows it. How'd the boss ever come up with it?"

"When he discovered this temple, he heard the villagers talking about it," Tamm replied.

There was some unintelligible conversation, and then the two thieves changed the subject.

"I have the second ruby," Tamm gloated. "Snatched it while the Hardys were in To Kor. Lucky the boss got wind of it in time to send me over and steal it. It's right here in my pocket where it's a lot safer than in McVay's secret pocket," he snickered.

Suddenly, a roaring sound in the sky caught the attention of Frank and Joe. The sound grew louder and a small plane flew out of a billowing bank of white clouds. The boys ducked behind an ancient statue and watched the craft approach. The pilot dipped a wing, circled the temple, and came down in the jungle not far away.

"He's obviously a member of the gang," Joe

muttered. "They must have hacked an airstrip out of the jungle."

The plane came to a stop and the engine was shut off. The sound of the door slamming told the Hardys that the pilot had left the cockpit. Soon they spotted him walking toward the temple, where he circled the wall and entered. He wore Western clothes, and when he shouted, "Hello? Anybody here?" the young detectives realized that he was an American.

"Everybody's here, Rob," Tamm replied from one of the windows. "Come on up."

The newcomer entered the temple and a moment later Tamm introduced him to Summers as Rob Ormand, who flew the gang's stolen rubies to Burma.

"I have a pilot's license to use the airport in Rangoon," Ormand explained. "And the Burmese government doesn't suspect a thing. Anyway, what's up? When you radioed me from Bangkok, you mentioned a ruby you were after. Have you got it?"

"Sure have! But I had another brilliant idea. I rounded up our gang so we can raid To Kor and get all the rubies at the Exchange. It'll all take place tomorrow."

"Okay, I'll be ready for the flight to Rangoon," the pilot promised. "I know a village where I can spend the night. I'll leave my plane here and wait for you to get here with the gems."

"Good," Tamm agreed. "See you tomorrow."

Ormand went out of the temple and the Hardys saw him retrace his steps through the jungle in the direction of the airstrip. Then he vanished between the trees.

Frank and Joe crouched in tense silence, waiting to hear more. But no one spoke for a while in the room below.

Joe rose to alleviate his cramped position, when suddenly his foot hit a small stone and propelled it through the doorway onto the stairs. It skidded off the landing and bounced down the steps.

"Somebody's up on the turret!" Summers shouted.

Feet pounded across the room below and up the stairs. The gang surged out onto the turret with Tamm in the lead. Frank and Joe retreated and stood with their backs to the wall. On the other side there was nothing but a straight drop to the flagstones below!

"It's the Hardys!" Tamm yelled. "We've got 'em cornered! Grab 'em!"

16 Prisoners of the Idol

The men charged furiously across the turret at the Hardys.

Frank felt behind his back for a stone to use as a weapon, and his fingers closed around a thick vine. Looking down, he saw that it led all the way to the ground. "This way, Joe!" he cried and vaulted over the parapet.

Joe came after him, barely evading Tamm's clutching fingers, and followed Frank along the temple wall. They could hear Tamm shouting angrily at the gang in Thai.

"We have a head start on them!" Joe said as he jumped to the ground. "Maybe we'll make it!"

But when the boys turned, they saw four

Thais with upraised machetes closing in on them! The men swung the wicked-looking long knives used for hacking paths through the jungle, and the blades whistled through the air with a threatening *swish!*

"I think we'd better stay where we are," Frank advised, his voice shaky.

The rest of the gang came down the stairs and rushed to the spot where the boys were being held. Tamm glared at them. "Ah, this time we have you for good!" he hissed.

"Right," Summers added. "Let's do 'em in now!"

Tamm shook his head and laughed maliciously. "That would be too easy on 'em. We'll let the idol do the job—slowly!"

He led the way to a small stone door at the rear of the building. The four men with machetes forced the Hardys to follow until they came to an enormous stone idol lying face down near the door.

Tamm rapped on the door with his knuckles. "It's stuck tight," he announced. "Hasn't been opened in centuries. And it's the only entrance to the room. We'll put these wise guys inside and leave 'em!"

"They might escape," Summers protested. "They're smart."

"That's where the idol comes in," Tamm declared. He gave the Thais an order in their own language. The gang lifted the stone idol, and, puffing and straining, they maneuvered it over to the wall and placed it with its back against the stone door.

The Hardys shuddered when they saw the face of the stone figure. The mouth was twisted into an evil leer, and the eyes were half-closed as if threatening anyone who might come near.

"Even if you got the door to move, which you can't, you couldn't push it open with the idol standing against it!" Tamm hissed in Frank's ear.

"How do we get in?" the boy asked.

Tamm smirked. "You'll see." Again, he spoke some words in Thai, then turned to Summers. "We're going to the throne room."

The Hardys were forced to accompany the gang up the stairs. Tamm ordered his men to move aside the throne, revealing a square hole underneath. Then he pushed the boys to the opening. They stared down into darkness so complete that they were unable to see the floor of the room below.

The Thais were about to shove the young detectives down when Tamm stopped them. "No, they might get knocked out right away if we do that," he said and tore two long, strong vines from the wall. With a grin he tied them around the boys' waists, then ordered the gang to lower the brothers into the hole.

Frank and Joe dangled helplessly in the air, twisting around and around until they dropped to the floor.

"Enjoy your demise," Tamm called, and the Thais on top pushed the throne back into its place on the dais.

Frank and Joe sat stunned for a moment. Then they removed the vines, took out their pencil flashlights, and peered around. They saw they were in a large, empty room made of stone blocks, with the ceiling much too high for them to reach.

"Even if we could get up there, we wouldn't be able to move the throne," Frank said dejectedly.

Joe tried the door. "Tamm's right. It won't budge. And with the idol standing against it outside, we're stuck!"

They moved into the center of the room, where Joe felt something slither over his shoe. He pointed the beam of his flashlight downward to the floor, and froze in horror.

He was looking at a cobra! The light caused the snake to rear up in an attacking position! Its hood spread wide at the neck as it swayed back and forth only inches from Joe's leg, ready to strike!

The Hardys knew from their outdoor training that the only defense against a poisonous snake that close was to remain still. Joe therefore stood as motionless as if he had been turned to stone. He felt a trickle of sweat run down the side of his face.

Frank watched in horror, for he could do nothing. Any sudden movement on his part, and the cobra might strike Joe! He felt his breath coming in short gasps.

The boys stood immobilized for what seemed like an eternity. Joe was beginning to feel that he could not last a moment longer when the cobra abruptly deflated its hood, lowered its head onto the floor, and crawled away into the darkness.

"I thought I was finished," Joe gasped.

"It's good you kept your cool," Frank mumbled, "or you would have been. And yet it's just a question of time. How long can we last in here trapped with a cobra?" He shivered as he spoke.

"Wait a minute!" Joe had a sudden idea. "If the cobra got in here, it must be able to get out! Maybe this place isn't as tight as Tamm thinks!"

Frank brightened. "You're right!" He shone his light around to pick up the cobra, and his beam followed it across the room to a corner, where it moved over a big pile of stone chips and vanished.

Approaching gingerly, the boys pointed their lights over the pile and saw the snake slithering through a hole between two stone blocks. The sinuous coils of the cobra wound through the hole, leaving a circle of daylight shining into the room from outside.

"The mortar in between the blocks is crumbling," Joe cried out. "Come on, let's go to work!"

Excitedly, they took steel probes from their detective kits and scraped away the mortar. After an hour of feverish effort, they managed to push one block back gradually until it gave way and tumbled to the ground.

Frank and Joe squeezed through the opening, covering their eyes with their hands until they got used to the light.

"Wow!" Frank exclaimed. "That was the closest call we've ever had!"

Joe nodded. "We have to get to To Kor before the gang," he said, trying to keep his voice steady. "We must warn the miners about the raid!"

"Right. But first let's make sure that no more stolen rubies get flown from here to Rangoon!"

The Hardys ran to the spot where they had seen the small plane land. They found enough of the jungle hacked away to provide an airstrip carpeted with a level expanse of grass and protected by tall trees growing all around. The plane stood at one end with the door to the cockpit locked.

"We can't get at the engine," Frank said, "and we don't have much time. So we'll have to knock out the propeller."

Seizing a heavy branch lying in the underbrush, he wielded it until he bent the propeller out of shape. Joe did the same to the flaps at the tail of the plane. They surveyed the disabled aircraft with satisfaction.

"Ormand won't be flying anywhere!" Joe observed. "Not unless he turns into a bird!"

Frank laughed. "Good work. Let's go!"

They plunged into the jungle and retraced the route they had taken on the way out. When they approached the stream they had crossed by jumping from rock to rock, they heard the sound of voices. Slipping silently through the jungle, the boys reached a point where they could see Tamm and his gang camped on the bank of the stream near the rocks.

Tamm spoke to the Thais, and then informed Summers, "I told them we'll stay here for an hour or so. We might as well have a quick snooze before pushing on."

They all lay down and soon were fast asleep.

Noiselessly, the Hardys stepped between the men and headed for the stream. They were next to Tamm when he began to stir! He pressed his hands against the ground and moved his head restlessly.

The boys froze in their tracks and stared apprehensively at him. If he wakes up, we've had it! Frank thought.

But Tamm rolled over on his side and went back to sleep. Frank and Joe hurried past, reached the stream, and started across. Suddenly Joe's foot came down on a wet, slippery rock, and he lost his balance!

17 The Tables Are Turned

Desperately, Joe threw out his arms, using them as stabilizers. He teetered over the rushing water, then regained his footing and leaped to the next rock. A moment later, he jumped onto the opposite bank beside Frank.

"If you'd have fallen in, those crooks would have heard the splash for sure!" Frank whispered.

"I know, that's why I didn't fall in!" Joe tried to make light of his near accident. "Come on, we'd better hurry."

The young detectives darted into the jungle and hastened along the route with which they were familiar. When darkness fell, they made occasional pauses to take a compass bearing by flashlight. The light disturbed birds and monkeys, and the Hardys were accompanied by an uproar of shrieking and chattering in the trees.

They reached To Kor at sunrise. Hurrying to Chao Mai's shack, they found him with Bo Dai. The two men had been up all night because they were too worried to sleep.

"Have you returned with the ruby?" Bo Dai asked sharply.

Frank shook his head. "No, but we think we can get it back today. Tamm and his gang are on their way here, and we heard him say that he's carrying the gem."

"They are planning to raid the Ruby Exchange," Joe spoke up.

"What!"

Quickly the Hardys told the men what they had overheard. "We can set a trap for the gang," Frank finished. "But we need the cooperation of the miners."

Bo Dai stood up and ran outside. He took a whistle from his pocket and blew three times. The piercing, high-pitched blasts brought the workers on a run.

"That's our emergency signal," the agent explained. "Everyone assembles instantly."

When the men were gathered, the Hardys talked to them, using Bo Dai as an interpreter.

Quickly they recounted what they knew about Tamm and his gang. At the end, the miners milled around muttering to one another. Several gave the boys angry looks.

"What's wrong?" Joe wondered aloud.

"They say they are suspicious of you," Bo Dai explained. "They ask how it is that you know so much about the criminals. They believe you may belong to the gang."

Joe was about to speak, when a loud explosion occurred in the jungle. A column of smoke rose into the sky. Chao Mai shouted something and ran toward it. The rest of the miners raced after him.

"Maybe the criminals intended to blow up the Exchange and their charge went off prematurely," Bo Dai cried out. He was about to follow the others when Frank laid a restraining hand on his arm.

"This could be a trap!" the boy warned. "Tamm may have ordered that explosion so that the miners would think the gang was out there!"

"He wants everybody out of To Kor while he and his crooks come and steal the rubies," Joe added.

"What shall we do?" the ruby agent wailed. "The thieves will get away before the miners come back!"

"No, they won't!" Frank declared. "Instead, we'll catch them red-handed. Do you have a key to the Ruby Exchange?"

"Of course. As an official agent of the government, I do."

"Good. Let's go there right now," Frank said. "We'll put the key into the lock from the outside and leave the door open. When our friends go in, we lock them up!"

Bo Dai's tense face broke into a wide grin. "Good idea!"

The trio set up their trap, then hid behind trees. A moment later Tamm and Summers arrived. The Thai members of the gang filed in after them.

"My plan worked!" Tamm chortled. "The explosion we set off will keep the miners away while we raid the place. If they come back too soon, we'll strong-arm 'em."

Summers pointed to the Exchange. "No need to blow out the door, either," he crowed. "The guy in charge must have forgotten to close it when the explosion went off. We can walk right in."

He stepped rapidly across the intervening area and entered the Ruby Exchange, closely followed by Tamm and the Thai crooks. As soon as they were inside, Frank ran over, slammed the door, and turned the key in the lock. Joe and Bo Dai rushed across and joined him at one of the windows, where they could see inside.

Consternation had broken out among the gang. Tamm rushed to the door and turned the handle. "It's locked!" he rasped. "But we have explosives. We can open it."

"Are you crazy?" Summers cried. "You'll blow us all to bits in this confined space!"

"How about the windows?"

"They're barred," Summers pointed out. Then he suddenly started to scream when he saw Bo Dai and the boys. "It was the Hardys! They got out of the temple and made it here ahead of us. They were the ones who set the trap!"

Tamm rushed to the window and stared in disbelief. "How did they ever get out of that room?"

"You see, we should have done them in right away!" Summers declared. "You and your bright ideas!"

The two crooks fell into a heated dispute. They were still wrangling when the ruby miners streamed back from the jungle. Quickly Bo Dai filled them in on what happened.

The men ran to the building and looked inside. They broke into loud cheers when they saw the would-be thieves penned up, then apologized for suspecting the Hardys, while Chao Mai went to call the police.

An hour later two officers arrived in a jeep. They took charge while the front door of the Ruby Exchange was unlocked and the crooks were brought out.

"Search Tamm," Joe advised. "He's got Chao Mai's ruby."

The jewel thief scowled furiously, but there was nothing he could do to stop the police. One of them found the giant ruby in his pocket and gave it back to the owner. Chao Mai accepted the brilliant gem with a tremendous sigh of relief.

Yet, under interrogation by the police, none of the criminals would talk.

Frank decided to use shock tactics. "Tell us about the Blue Triangle and the Crimson Flame!" he said suddenly to Tamm.

The jewel thief looked startled. "So, you know about that too!" he burst out. Regaining his composure, he added sarcastically, "But if you have to ask me, you don't know everything. Well, you figure it out if you guys are so smart!"

That was all he would say. Just then a large police patrol rolled into To Kor, and the crooks were herded into a van and taken to Bangkok.

"The Thai criminals will be in prison for some time," Bo Dai commented. "No doubt

Tamm and Summers will be extradited to America for trial. The American pilot, Ormand, will be arrested and his plane will be impounded."

Chao Mai interrupted with a flow of words.

"He thanks you for recovering his ruby," Bo Dai declared. "And he wants to know if you are still interested in buying it."

"Yes, we are," Frank said.

"Then let us go and discuss the matter."

Inside Chao Mai's shack, the miner placed the ruby on the table, where it glowed and sparkled. He agreed to sell it to the Hardys for less than fifty thousand dollars in appreciation of what they had done for him, and Bo Dai wrote out a check for the amount. Frank put the gem into a hidden compartment of his detective kit, and then the meeting broke up.

On the way back to Bangkok, Frank and Joe decided that they should return to the United States.

After getting a good rest at their hotel, the boys caught a plane for Los Angeles. The California coast was in sight when Frank summed up what he had been thinking all along.

"Joe, I have a hunch that the Crimson Flame is still in Arizona!"

157

18 *Signals on the Range*

"What makes you think so?" Joe asked.

"The boss of the gang must be close to Mr. McVay to have known McVay was going to New York. I think the kingpin lives in Arizona!"

When the Hardys reached Los Angeles, Joe called the rancher, gave him a brief report, and was told that Jupe would meet them at the Flagstaff airport.

The young cowboy was waiting for them when they came through the gate with their bags. "Perkins is still missing," he revealed. "No one knows where he is."

"I suppose he found another job," Frank said casually, concealing the fact that the foreman's other job was working for jewel thieves.

At the ranch, Jupe dropped the Hardys at the big house and continued on to the bunkhouse. Frank and Joe were admitted by Wilbur, who showed them into Mr. McVay's study. Hunched in his chair behind his desk, his eyes round with excitement, the rancher jabbered with delight when Frank gave him the ruby.

"Excellent! Excellent!" he chirped. "By the way, Bo Dai phoned me from Bangkok. He told me how you boys captured Tamm and his gang. He also said something about an American pilot who was arrested in the jungle. I gather he couldn't get his plane into the air."

"He had propeller trouble," Frank stated with a grin. "We fixed his plane so he couldn't take off."

"Good work!" McVay beamed. Then he became solemn. "What about the Crimson Flame?"

"We heard Tamm say that the Blue Triangle has it," Joe explained. "He's the boss of the gang, someone with a blue triangle on his hand."

"Sheriff Gomez has a dragnet out for Perkins," McVay said. "He would know who the Blue Triangle is. But so far there's no sign of my foreman."

"We'll keep looking for him," Joe promised. "And for the Crimson Flame."

The Hardys returned to the bunkhouse and called Chet and Biff at the Jomo ranch. The four agreed to meet at the main trail. Frank and Joe saddled up and rode there without delay.

Soon their friends arrived. "How was your trip?" Chet asked. "Did you find the Crimson Flame?"

"No," Frank replied, "but we bought another ruby and caught the thieves. The only one still missing is the boss." Quickly he told what happened.

"You did a great job," Biff said, impressed. "And I'm sure you'll find the gang leader yet!"

"How did things go here?" Joe asked. "Any action?"

"Nothing," Chet said.

"We learned the real meaning of the Blue Triangle," Frank spoke up and explained the symbol. If you see anyone with one of those things tattooed on his hand, let us know."

Biff nodded. "So far we haven't noticed anyone. But we'll look."

"Good. We'll check at McVay's, then we'll talk to you tonight."

The four boys broke up and returned to their ranches. Frank and Joe surreptitiously checked the McVay cowboys as they came into the bunkhouse. But no one had a blue triangle on his hand.

Later, Joe called Biff. After a short conversation, he put down the phone and shook his head, indicating that their friends' search had been fruitless, too.

The next day, Mr. McVay asked the boys to check on the fence again. They rode past the corrals and noticed that Barson and Marti were missing. "I don't know where they are," Jupe replied to their question as he led a wild horse from one corral to another.

The Hardys toured the fence without seeing any broken wires or uprooted posts, and the longhorns were undisturbed.

"No rustlers operating here today," Joe declared. "Mr. McVay—" He stopped when a bright light glinted from the ridge in the desert. They saw a horseman wearing a bandana over his face and a floppy Thailand-style hat on his head. He kept turning a mirror from side to side, catching the sun's rays in flashes of light.

"It's the mysterious rider!" Frank said excitedly. "He's sending a message in semaphore to somebody on the other side of the range!"

The Hardys knew how to read semaphore signaling, which they often used in their detective work. It enabled them to send messages to each other by blinking their flashlights or waving their handkerchiefs. It came in handy when they had no other means of communicating.

Watching the mysterious rider flashing his mirror on the ridge, they read his message letter-by-letter: "M-A-I-N T-R-A-I-L T-W-E-N-T-Y M-I-N-U-T-E-S."

"Let's go after him!" Frank exclaimed.

Joe was already galloping toward the fence, which they both vaulted over in great jumps. They pounded across the desert toward the ridge, but the mysterious rider spotted them. He turned his horse and leaped down the opposite side. By the time they got there, he was gone.

"We've lost him again!" Frank cried in frustration as he reined in his mount.

"We can still go to the main trail and see what's up," Joe pointed out.

"Right." The boys rode through the woods, tied their horses to a tree near the trail, and crouched behind a bush to see what would happen.

A truck came up. It was the same one they had seen when they had shadowed Barson and Marti. The same driver was in the cab. He made a turn so wide that he nearly ran over the bush behind which the Hardys were hiding. Then he parked and turned off the ignition.

"Could be the rustlers are starting up again," Joe whispered. "This might be their truck. I'll alert Sheriff Gomez. You keep watch here, okay?"

Frank nodded and Joe sneaked over to his horse. He took a walkie-talkie from his saddle bag and called the sheriff's patrol car. Gomez promised to be right over.

Joe rejoined Frank and the two continued their vigil. Some time later they heard the low mooing of cattle. Three longhorns bearing the Jomo brand lumbered down the trail. Barson and Marti were herding them toward the truck. A third man rode after them.

"It's Wat Perkins!" Frank gasped.

19 *Main Trail Melee*

"Get 'em aboard the truck!" Perkins said to Barson and Marti.

The two cowboys pulled a ramp from the back of the vehicle and lowered one end to the ground. With Perkins's help, they prodded the longhorns up.

"Now go to Flagstaff pronto!" Perkins ordered when they had finished. "The Blue Triangle will take care of the money."

As the driver started the motor, Joe heard hoofbeats behind them. He whirled around and saw Chet and Biff galloping up the trail.

"Frank! With those two to help us we can stop these guys!" he cried out. "Let's go!"

The Hardys charged from behind the bush and dashed toward the truck. The driver started, but Joe kicked a large log under the front wheels, bringing the truck to a jarring stop.

The three men jumped out of the truck and a battle royal erupted. But it lasted only a short time. The scream of a police siren echoed over the area. Three patrol cars raced to the scene, and Sheriff Gomez and his deputies leaped out and joined in the fray.

At the sight of the police, Perkins had run to his horse and jumped in the saddle, and he was now galloping up the trail.

Frank instantly chased him. After a few minutes, he had narrowed the gap between them to a few yards. He let his mount have its head while he played out his lasso with both hands. When he had the rope zooming in circles, he tossed it over Perkins's shoulders and dragged him from the saddle.

The fall stunned the rustler long enough for the young detective to jump down and tie the man's hands behind his back. Perkins's horse had turned and was walking toward them. Then it stopped and began nibbling the grass.

"All right, Perkins, get back on!" Frank ordered.

Cowed, the man put his foot in the stirrup and Frank pushed him into the saddle. He remounted himself and led his captive down the trail at the end of his lasso. They reached the truck, where the sheriff was talking to Chet.

"We saw Barson and Marti on the Jomo range. They had no business there, so we decided to watch them," Chet said.

"Next thing we knew," Biff took up the story, "they separated three longhorns from the herd and drove them to the fence. Then they cut the barbed wire and went to the main trail."

"We followed them, and came upon Frank and Joe," Chet added. "And between the four of us we got 'em!"

"What do you have to say to that?" Gomez asked the crooks in a stern voice. "You were caught red-handed stealing cattle! You've been rustling Mr. Jomo's longhorns all along, haven't you? Are you working for somebody else?"

The prisoners stared at the ground with guilty looks on their faces, but made no reply.

"Sheriff, we can tell you one thing about them," Joe said. "They were taking the cattle to Flagstaff. They must have a dishonest buyer there."

Gomez shook his head to show his surprise. "I've been concentrating on Phoenix because both I and Mr. Jomo thought it would be the more likely place. It's good you boys discovered the Flagstaff angle. Flagstaff is a much smaller city. The buyer won't be hard to find."

The Hardys explained their part in capturing the criminal band, beginning with the message flashed in semaphore by the mysterious rider.

"*He* arranged this caper," Frank stated. "He told his gang to be at the main trail in twenty minutes, and that's where we found them. Perkins and the Blue Triangle would take care of the money. We have to find him and the mysterious rider, unless they are one and the same person."

"Let me know if you discover any clues," the sheriff said, then ordered two of his deputies to take the stolen longhorns back to the Jomo ranch. The rest of the officers escorted the rustlers and their truck to police headquarters. Chet and Biff remounted and rode to the Jomo ranch, leading behind them the horses ridden by Perkins, Barson, and Marti. The boys had seen these horses in the Jomo stable, and knew that the crooks had stolen them.

"I'll report to Mr. Jomo that the rustling ring is finished," Sheriff Gomez told the Hardys. "He'll be pleased with the good work you've done."

Joe grinned. "And we'll tell Mr. McVay that three of his cowboys are in the lockup."

Riding back to the McVay ranch, Frank had an idea. He mentioned it to Joe, who was all for it. They left their horses in the stable and went to the big house to explain it to McVay.

"We'll set a trap and see if the thief who stole the Crimson Flame walks into it," Frank said. "He sure wants the second ruby we just bought. So we'll give him a chance to get into the vault again."

McVay shook his head doubtfully. "I can't risk putting the gem into the vault. I have it now in my bank deposit box."

Frank nodded. "Leave it there. All you have to do is *say* it's in the vault. Then we'll hide there and ambush the crook!"

"But he won't dare to come in when the house is full of people!"

"We'll see that it's empty," Joe took up the plan. "The thief got the Crimson Flame because he knew no one was here after the tornado hit. This time we'll put a smoke bomb in the attic. You'll order the servants out, saying the house is on fire. That will give the thief his chance to get in, and we'll be waiting for him!"

McVay became excited. "You boys are very clever. I'll do it! I'll tell everybody I know that the second ruby is in my vault in the basement!"

"We'll spread the word at the bunkhouse," Joe declared. "And we'll get Chet and Biff to do the same at the Jomo place. In a few days, everyone will know, including the thief."

The Hardys bought the necessary material for a smoke bomb, and two days later they slipped into the attic while no one was looking and placed the finished item near one of the windows. When smoke began to billow out, they raised a cry of "Fire!"

On their way downstairs, they heard the rancher ordering his staff out into the front yard. "The house is on fire!" he yelled.

Lingering behind as if to see that he was the last person in the house, McVay met the Hardys and escorted them into the basement. Snapping the secret switch to the burglar alarm, he spun the dial of the combination lock and opened the vault door. The overhead light flashed on, the boys went in, and the light went off as McVay shut the door and locked it. Then he put the burglar alarm back on and left.

Frank sat on the floor with his back against the wall. "We might as well be comfortable," he commented. "We don't know how long we'll have to wait."

"Too bad we didn't bring our sleeping bags,"

Joe quipped, trying to see through the tiny window in the vault door. But it was completely dark in the basement.

Suddenly he gasped. "Frank!" he whispered. "Someone's coming down. The light just went on!"

Frank came up to his brother and peered through the small opening. He saw Wilbur reach under the stairs and turn off the burglar alarm, then walk to the back of the basement. A sliding noise told the boys he had unbolted the rear door. Wilbur returned and spun the dial of the combination lock until the tumblers fell into place. Leaving the vault door unlocked, he went upstairs again and switched off the light.

"He's got everything ready for the thief!" Joe said. "I can't wait to see who it is!"

Ten minutes later, they heard a noise at the back door. The boys got to their feet and flattened themselves against the wall. Their hearts pounded from the excitement they felt.

Footsteps crossed the basement in the darkness. A small flashlight went on, its narrow beam playing across the vault door. A hand pushed up the catch, the door opened, and the overhead light went on. A man came into the vault, approached the jewel case, took a key from his pocket, and unlocked the case.

Concentrating on what he was doing, he

never noticed the Hardys. He lifted the lid and stared in disbelief at the empty black velvet where the ruby was supposed to be. Frank and Joe stepped forward on either side of him.

"Hello, Mr. Jomo!" Frank said.

20 *The Blue Triangle*

The man whirled around and stared at the boys in utter shock. Then he started to bolt for the door.

Frank and Joe quickly blocked the way and a short melee ensued. Jomo fought desperately to get away, but he was no match for the strong, agile boys, who subdued him and tied his hands behind his back with Joe's belt. Then they took him upstairs.

While Joe led the man into Mr. McVay's study, Frank went outside to tell the rancher that he could let his people into the house again.

"It's all over," he said quietly, "and we have your man."

"You—you caught him!" McVay was thunderstruck. "Who is he?"

"Come and see for yourself," Frank said.

When McVay entered the study, he stared in surprise. "Now wait a minute, boys," he said. "What's this all about?"

"He's the thief," Joe said. "Sorry, Mr. McVay, I know you trusted this man, but—"

"I—I can't believe it!" the rancher said, his face showing a tumult of emotions. He let himself sink into the chair and sat still for a few moments.

"My friend," he murmured. "My friend!"

"He only pretended to be your friend," Frank observed. "When you told him you were going to New York to get the Crimson Flame, he phoned Tamm and told him about the secret pocket in your jacket. That's why Tamm attacked you in the subway."

Joe added more details. "When Tamm reported his failure in New York, Jomo told him to come to Arizona to figure out how to steal the ruby from the vault. But when the tornado hit the house, Jomo rushed in himself and took the Crimson Flame while everybody was outside. He handed it to Perkins just before we saw them through the window. That's why Jomo asked Sheriff Gomez to search him. He wanted to make it look good."

"You're crazy!" Jomo scoffed. "How could I get into the basement? The door was bolted!"

"The same way you did just now," Frank replied evenly. "Mr. McVay, sent for Wilbur. He knows what happened."

McVay ordered the butler to report to the study. While they were waiting, Sheriff Gomez arrived. "I heard on the patrol car radio that your house was on fire," he said. "But I see it's all under control now."

When McVay told him what was happening, Gomez responded grimly, "We'd better get to the bottom of this!"

Wilbur came into the study. The Hardys described how the butler had turned off the burglar alarm and unbolted the back door while he thought the house was on fire.

"I just wanted to make sure anyone trapped by the fire could get out of the house by the basement door," Wilbur defended himself.

"We saw you open the lock on the vault," Frank charged.

"That's impossible! I don't know the combination!"

McVay intervened. "Wilbur's right. I always make him stay at the top of the basement stairs when I open the vault. It's too far for anyone to see the numbers of the combination when I spin the dial."

An idea struck Joe. "I know how he did it!" he exclaimed. "I'll be right back!"

He left the study and went up the stairs to the next floor.

"Mr. McVay, after the tornado, Wilbur told you the house might collapse so you'd get everybody out," Frank theorized. "He phoned Jomo that the coast was clear. We nearly fouled up everything for him when we went inside. But he fooled us into giving the kitchen a special inspection. While we were there he sneaked down into the basement, turned off the burglar alarm, unbolted the back door, and opened the vault lock for Jomo."

The rancher nodded sadly. "It all makes sense now."

"Yes. He also tried to get rid of us," Frank went on, "by turning on the gas, dropping the silver tray on Joe, and pushing Joe out the attic window."

McVay blinked his eyes. "But I never told Wilbur you were detectives! I never told anybody out here!"

"Word got here from New York after we tangled with Tamm at the hotel," Frank explained. "Tamm phoned Jomo, and Jomo told Wilbur. A neat triple play!"

Joe returned while Frank was speaking. He held small binoculars in his hand.

"Wilbur, you're an amateur bird-watcher. You used your binoculars to read the numbers of the combination lock. Mr. McVay never knew you were spying on him from the top of the stairs."

"And you stole Mr. McVay's key to the jewel case and had a duplicate made," Frank inferred. "You gave Jomo the duplicate and returned the original to Mr. McVay's key ring."

The evidence presented by the Hardys made Wilbur collapse in a chair, his head hopelessly buried in his hands.

"You can't prove any of this!" Jomo snarled.

"I bet I can prove even more," Frank said. "Joe, watch this guy while I untie his hands."

The boys walked over to Jomo and Frank took the leather belt off, then began to work on Jomo's bandage.

"Are you crazy?" the man screamed. "You can't do that! The doctor put that on—"

"I don't think so, Mr. Jomo," Frank said. "*You* put it on to hide the blue triangle on your hand when you heard we were coming to Arizona. You wanted to avoid any questions about it."

McVay stared at the symbol Frank uncovered on his neighbor's hand. "That's—that's incredible!" he said. "You've caught the Blue Triangle!"

"I think we also caught the mysterious rider,
Joe spoke up.

"And the head of the rustling operation,"
Frank added. "Mr. Jomo had Perkins, Barson,
and Marti steal his own cattle to distract the
sheriff's attention from the jewel robberies."

Sheriff Gomez looked grim. "Now I get it,
Jomo. You wanted me to look in Phoenix for the
crooked cattle dealer to send me off on a wild-
goose chase. It would keep me busy and you
could sell your longhorns in Flagstaff without
any trouble."

"You can't prove any of this," Jomo repeated.
"Besides, you said yourself that the mysterious
rider had black hair and piercing eyes. I have
brown hair and wear glasses."

"You wore a wig and left your glasses at
home," Frank concluded. "Sheriff Gomez, if
you get a warrant and search his house, you'll
find another hat from Thailand just like the one
I grabbed from the mysterious rider. He bought
them at the Thieves Market in Bangkok!"

"You'll probably also find the Crimson Flame
and perhaps other stolen jewels," Joe said. "I
bet Jomo wasn't too happy when we suggested
that he hire Chet and Biff. The last thing he
needed was people poking into his affairs. But
if he had declined, we'd have become suspicious, so he went along with it."

Sheriff Gomez called his deputies, who came and took the thieves to jail. Another officer arrived sometime later with a search warrant for Jomo's house, and a thorough inspection of the neighboring ranch revealed a collection of stolen jewels, including the Crimson Flame, and a hat made in Bangkok.

Mr. McVay was happy to get his ruby back, and commended the boys on the wonderful job they had done. "Would you like to spend the rest of the summer here?" he asked. "You wouldn't have to work, either!"

"Thanks, Mr. McVay," Frank said. "But we'll have to go back home. Secretly he was eager to start working on another mystery. Soon his wish was to be fulfilled when the Hardys were asked to investigate *Cave-In*.

"All right," the rancher said. "Book a flight tomorrow and Jupe'll take you to the airport."

Joe grinned. "I'm so glad it turned out he wasn't a crook after all," he said. "Jupe's a nice guy. I really got to like him."

"So did I," Frank said.